D0770661

HAUNTED
BOULDER

Ghostly Tales From the Foot of the Flatirons

Roz Brown
Ann Alexander Leggett

WS
LP

White Sand Lake Press

For information write: White Sand Lake Press, 750 S. 41st St., Boulder, CO, 80305 or e-mail: hauntedboulder@hotmail.com

Library of Congress Control Number: 2002108870
ISBN: 0966565428

Contents

Contents

Chapter 13
Short But Spooky

For my Aunt Lorraine,
unsurpassed in the art of storytelling.

❖ *Roz*

For Nicholas and Jordan,
the inspiration for it all.

❖ *Ann*

Acknowledgments

Special thanks to: all of the homeowners, who have allowed us to tour their homes and learn about their resident ghosts; the staff of Psychic Horizons, for their support from the very beginning and their interpretations of Boulder's spirits; the staff and volunteers of Historic Boulder, past and present, who opened their files for us and provided stories and recollections, and generally paved the way for this book; Kathryn Barth and Diana Beer, for their unbridled enthusiasm and unending support; Wendy Hall and all the librarians and volunteers at Boulder's Carnegie Library for Local History, for their expertise and for helping us find hidden gems of information; historians Jane Valentine Barker, Sybil Downing, and Silvia Pettem, for their invaluable information about Boulder's past; reporters at the *Daily Camera*, *Colorado Daily*, *Campus Press*, and *Boulder Magazine*, for keeping Boulder's ghosts stories alive; Linda Cornett, for her excellent reporting; the Boulder History Museum's DeAnne Butterfield; Tom Alexander, for his bits of literary wisdom; Jordan Leggett, for her many hours of research help; Scott Leggett, for reading the galleys over and over until he couldn't see straight; Sara Sheldon at White Sand Lake Press, for holding our hands and leading the way; and to our families, for being patient and understanding while we undertook yet another project in our crazy lives!

foreword

Ghost stories have been around for centuries, yet we never seem to tire of reading about things that go bump in the night, or day. Boulder's rich history and colorful ghosts certainly made this book fun to write. The stories found here are based on folklore, hearsay, old memories, and documentation that can be found in public records. The ghost stories themselves are as accurate as we have been able to determine. Some names have been changed to protect the homeowners. We ask that the home and business owners not be contacted in any way. For additional information, please contact the authors at: *hauntedboulder@hotmail.com.*

At this time of dark and night,
spirits often give a fright.
We call upon the ancient dead,
circling now around our head.
Bring the blessings from before,
while we stand with open door.
Ancient spirits hear us now,
peace and love do we avow.

❖

THE ARNETT-FULLEN HOUSE

Chapter 1

THE ARNETT-FULLEN HOUSE

Designated as a local landmark in 1990, visitors enter the Arnett-Fullen House today and find the offices of Historic Boulder. But within the confines of these walls are other visitors, those from long ago.

Tucked away at 646 Pearl Street, the Arnett-Fullen House seems to beckon to the passersby. A curious Victorian in miniature, the little yellow house with the French mansard tower and gabled roof sits back from the street on a corner lot, surrounded on two sides by a most intricate wrought-iron fence. Constructed with the finest materials of the day, the house was built in 1877 by Willamette Arnett, a flamboyant businessman who delighted in owning what would become a city showplace. Nothing like it existed in Boulder at the time.

Will Arnett came to Colorado as a child in 1859, his family lured to the area by the gold strikes near Pikes Peak. His father, Anthony Arnett, had immigrated to the United States from France in 1828. An astute businessman, the senior Arnett had interests in a variety of local ventures including mining and real estate, and was one of the University of Colorado's earliest contributors of both land and funds. He owned over 200 acres of land in the area on which he ran horses and cattle. His holdings extended from what is now Columbia Cemetery to the center of the CU campus, south to Baseline, and all the way west to Gregory Canyon. He also owned several lots on Pearl Street where he eventually built the Arnett Hotel. Well-respected and known about town as an honest man, Anthony Arnett was a true pioneer of the city. His family included nine children. Will was one of only four who survived to adulthood.

Will had the business interests of his father but unfortunately not the success. As a matter of fact, local historians have noted that the two were often complete opposites. Married twice with two children, Will was commonly described as flashy and showy. He was a walking picture of flamboyance, right down to the ten-dollar gold pieces he wore as buttons on several of his suit coats. As a result, nothing was too ornate for Mr. Arnett as he set out to build his home and livery on Pearl Street. The finest craftsmen in the area were hired and no costs were spared. Designed by George E. King, a prominent local architect, the layout of the 1,885 square foot house hasn't changed much since 1877 and still includes a parlor with a large bay window on the lower floor, a dining room, a family bedroom, a servant's bedroom, a kitchen, pantry, and a china closet. A bathroom with hot and cold running water set the townspeople abuzz as it was a first for Boulder. Faux painting and ornate floral designs still adorn the entry hall and parlor. Four small bedrooms make up the upper level. For the cost it was on the smallish side, but what it lacked in size, it made up for in elegance.

In February of 1877, the *Boulder County News* wrote this about William Arnett's new home:

"The exterior of Will Arnett's new residence on west Pearl is so nearly completed as to show the architectural beauty of the building in which it excels any residence ever before erected in Boulder. Mr. Arnett delights in the beautiful, is always ornamenting his grounds, and even his stables. The entrance to his livery stable is painted and gilded till it looks like an art gallery. But this new residence is his pet ornament and the gem of the city."

One of the focal points of the interior of the home is the narrow winding stairway rising to the upper floor which is visible immediately upon entering. Wide enough for only one person to pass at a time, it is framed with an exquisite black walnut balustrade complete with a stunning rosewood and bird's-eye maple inlay. It is on the bend of the stairway that one of the home's spirits is most often seen.

Building costs of the home were said to total $4,000, almost double what a similarly sized home should have cost at that time. Will spent $1,500 on the ornate wrought-iron fence alone, having it shipped by wagon train in pieces to Boulder from Pittsburgh. The house certainly brought notoriety to Mr. Arnett along with a great deal of debt. Construction liens on the home began to accumulate and financial woes caused his business ventures to falter. Will headed for the Northwest in the 1890s hoping to strike it rich in the Klondike Gold Rush. He died in Dawson City, Yukon Territory, in 1901.

Historical records and local reports vary on the actual dates of occupation of the home's next few residents. It is believed that Eliza Jane Fullen bought the Arnett House in the early 1900s. Eliza was the widow of Hiram Fullen, a Boulder miner, with whom she had three sons. She rented out the gingerbread house for several years before moving in with her mother, sister, and children. She spent her last years in poor health, resting in the small bedroom on the main floor with her sister Lilly at her side. After Eliza's death, Lilly became the caretaker and main resident of the house until she moved into a local nursing home. The Arnett-Fullen House began to fall into disrepair.

In the 1960s, one of Eliza's sons, Hiram Fullen, Jr., moved in, and with his wife set about restoring the house to its original splendor. The task was not an easy one. The balustrade of the stairwell had been painted black, completely hiding the stunning woodwork, and in some rooms up to fourteen layers of wallpaper adorned the walls. Painstakingly they restored room after room until the grand house blossomed under their care.

Designated as a local landmark in 1990, visitors enter the Arnett-Fullen home today and find the offices of Historic Boulder. But within the confines of these walls are other visitors, those from long ago. It's not clear exactly when the ghost activity started or how many years it goes back. As Historic Boulder's executive director from December, 1998, to June, 2000, Alan Hafer felt the spirits on several occasions, most often during the day as opposed to the night. Office staff jokingly referred to "the ghost" whenever office snafus and computer failures occurred. But it soon became apparent that the equipment glitches happened at moments that were just too coincidental to be accidental. The staff during Alan's tenure believed one of the spirits they were sensing was that of Will Arnett. Items disappearing into thin air overnight would invoke desk-clearing searches the next morning to no avail. Once, when furniture was being moved in the offices, the staff joked that Will would not be happy with the change. At the exact moment of the comment, a window shade fell from its mountings. Some staff members described sudden temperature shifts in a room or the feeling of someone being in the room with them when clearly they were alone.

Alan Hafer recalls a story that further convinced him that there were active spirits in the Arnett-Fullen house. "Four months after I started at Historic Boulder, I was going through my desk and I found a box labeled 'Jack's Bones.' No one in the office knew what they were and we all laughed about a box with such a name. Finally, we decided that they were bones that archeologist Jack Smith had dug up at an old Boulder stage station. We cautiously opened the box and found what appeared to be an ancient pig and deer bone. I set the box on the table in the front office so it could be returned to Jack. But overnight the box disappeared. We tore the office apart the next morning but it was nowhere to be found. We never did find those bones. Just as they appeared in my desk, they disappeared. Will has them someplace." Later it was established that no one on the staff had sent them out or taken them. They were never seen again.

With its rich history and resident spirits, the Arnett-Fullen home was a perfect candidate for Historic Boulder's Spirit Tour. On a visit to the house prior to the tour, Mary Bell Nyman, director of Boulder's Psychic Horizons, immediately sensed the spirit of a girl on the staircase when she first entered the house to do an interpretation. "She was standing on the stairway and she appeared to be approximately thirteen years old," Mary Bell says. "She was wearing a white-ribbed blouse and she was quite delighted to be noticed. She wanted people to feel her energy."

The ghost of the girl on the stairs is the most well-known spirit in the house and perhaps in the city. On the night of the tour, as visitors entered the home, Mary Bell was surprised that the spirit of the girl stayed on the steps the entire night. Her energy was evident by a feeling of cold that the visitors could actually run their hands through. "She clearly loved the attention," Mary Bell says. "She had a positive, happy energy."

During the tour, a visitor took several color photos of the house as Mary Bell spoke. When she saw the developed photos, she threw away the one of the stairway thinking it was simply overexposed because it had a white blotchy patch. Later, when she realized that the overexposure could have something to do with the spirit, she retrieved the photo from the trash. At second glance, the energy had revealed itself on the film, winding up the stairway.

But who is the girl on the stairs? Alan Hafer had heard stories of a woman who died of pneumonia in the home. According to Hafer, her weeping, wheezing, and crying could be heard throughout the house. Her death was quite prolonged and very painful. Hafer feels the spirit on the stairs may be the woman returning at an innocent age.

According to the folks at Historic Boulder, another spirit lurks in the home as well. This presence, that of an older man, has been felt on many occasions by the office staff who sense his spirit in the southeast corner of the old dining room. Some have refused to sit in that area of the home because they felt uneasy. "I immediately sensed a heavier energy in the back," Mary Bell says, "very much like that of an older, gruff man, perhaps a disapproving father." After talking to the Historic Boulder staff after the tour, Mary Bell made the connection of the spirit to Anthony Arnett, Will's father, who was known as being very upset by his son's lifestyle. Others believe the ghost is that of a CU professor who lived in the house with his young student wife, causing quite a scandal at the time. He was said to have died in the house. An area of cold air frequently surrounds his spirit.

Mary Bell's interpretation of the spirits in the house answered questions for the staff at Historic Boulder and confirmed their suspicions. "It wasn't scary for them in the least," Mary Bell says. "It was a validation of what they had been sensing for quite some time."

Although a direct connection to the girl on the stairs cannot be made to the history of the home, she might be the spirit of the woman who died of pneumonia in the home or perhaps that of Eliza Fullen. And it seems likely that the gruff gentleman in the back of the home could be the spirit of Anthony Arnett. One thing is for certain, all of the spirits in the Arnett-Fullen house are still very much alive. ❖

Photo by Ann Alexander Leggett

THE GHOST OF WILLIAM TULL

Chapter 2

THE GHOST OF WILLIAM TULL

To their horror, they saw the image of a man hanging by the neck from a cottonwood tree. Unable to comprehend what they were seeing, they moved closer but the vision of the man drifted away.

The events that unfolded on a warm summer evening in June, 1867, are the makings for Boulder's oldest ghost story. Only the winding banks of Boulder Creek near the Broadway bridge can tell the true tale of William Tull and his demise. His spirit didn't rest for many, many years, that much is known for sure.

Legend has it that twenty-six-year-old William Tull was a good kid. Raised with Chief Niwot's tribe of Arapaho Indians, Tull, who was originally from Ohio, became an adopted member of the band as they roamed the West. When the Sand Creek battle of 1864 nearly decimated the tribe and killed its chief, Tull moved into the town of Boulder to look for employment. He found work as a ranch hand on the north Boulder spread of James Tourtellote. Despite his move, his friendship with the remaining members of the Arapaho endured, and he frequently visited them as they moved from camp to camp.

Tull worked hard for Tourtellote, and one summer day, having earned some time off, he asked his employer for the use of two horses to visit Arapaho friends camped at the Cache la Poudre near Fort Collins. (Some historians say that Tull was off to visit his Cheyenne bride.) Tourtellote granted his request and with one horse saddled for riding and the other packed with supplies, Tull headed out on his trip. His first stop was Burlington, a heavily used stage stop south of what is now known as Longmont. There he bought groceries and continued on his way, arriving at the camp the next day to the delight of the tribe.

Tull had apparently promised Tourtellote that he would return on a specific date. When that time passed, rumors of horse theft spread and a posse was formed. Trackers followed Tull's path north to Burlington and then on to the Indian camp where he surrendered quietly. According to legend, the tribe's chief told the posse that Tull meant to leave earlier, but had only recently recovered his horses which had run away with the tribe's wild herd. The explanation fell on deaf ears.

Tull was escorted into Boulder by the trackers and was placed under arrest in a room guarded by Deputy Sheriff Anderson. Apparently the town had no jail at that time, so Tull and his guard holed-up in a room above the blacksmith shop. Tempers ran high that night and soon a mob formed. Storming the blacksmith shop in the dark of night, they wrestled Tull from the deputy and led him to the banks of the creek. Throwing a rope over the low limb of a cottonwood tree, they hanged William Tull for a crime for which he had not been tried, a crime many came to believe he had not even committed. After Tull's death it was revealed that Tourtellote had probably sold him the horses. Rumor has it that proof of the sale was found among Tull's effects after his death.

The citizens of Boulder awoke the next morning to witness what was Boulder's first and possibly only lynching. As he hung from the cottonwood, William Tull's feet scraped the rocky ground below as he slowly suffocated during the night. It was a tortuous death. An uproar among the town's citizens ensued. The Arapaho tribe, upon hearing of Tull's death, threatened revenge. Fearing an Indian attack, the townspeople built a fort at the rear of what eventually became the First National Bank. The threat was never carried out.

While his grave was being dug, Tull's body was laid in the home of Ephriam Pound, located just east of the town's dairy. Citizens, including school children and their teachers, crowded the home to view his corpse. He was finally laid to rest on the slope of the Pioneer Cemetery, also called Lovers' Hill Cemetery on Sunset Hill.

The cemetery, which was used from approximately 1867-1870, held the remains of about twenty-four individuals, some of whom were later moved to the Columbia Cemetery. The main plot was located on the top of the hill, the pauper section was down on the slope. The only cemetery in Boulder at the time, it was nothing more than a wind-swept bluff overlooking town. There were few headstones or markers and citizens of the town were outraged at the disrespect shown the dead. Most of the graves were eventually moved to the Columbia Cemetery on Ninth Street.

In 1935, local historian Martin Parsons wrote of his experiences in the cemetery as a young boy, indicating that the story of Tull's lynching persisted in local folklore for more than fifty years after he was hanged and laid to rest in 1867.

"I met Granville Berkeley in the cemetery one summer and he showed me the grave of William Tull. He had marked the grave with three large cobblestones. Tull's grave was the farthest down the slope. There were several graves higher up. The last time I was there in 1924, I counted twenty-two graves on the top of the hill but couldn't locate a grave on the slope of the hill."

In 1940, the city of Boulder, not knowing that graves still existed in the area, unearthed the skeletons of an adult and a child while doing road work. There is no record of Tull's remains ever being moved to the Columbia Cemetery.

With his death by hanging, Tull's story was far from over. It is said that after the lynching his unhappy spirit rose to meet a Boulder judge and a friend as they walked along the creek. To their horror, they saw the image of a man hanging by the neck from a cottonwood tree. Unable to comprehend what they were seeing, they moved closer to the tree but the vision of the man drifted away. The ghostly figure carried a rope and motioned towards its mouth as if it was in pain. According to the men, the apparition then disappeared into the evening light.

William Tull's ghost was seen a few days later by a local constable and again by a doctor, both of whom witnessed a man hanging from a tree limb, fading from sight as they approached. Additional sightings reported Tull's ghost approaching people walking along the creek and motioning as if asking for help in removing the rope around his neck. The story of the ghost quickly spread through town.

As joggers and bicyclists cruise along the creek path today they are most likely unaware of the events of that fateful night in June of 1867. Traffic rolls by on Broadway and life in the town, now a city, moves at a fast clip. Perhaps the restless spirit of William Tull has finally found peace, or maybe not. ❖

WALTER

Chapter 3

WALTER

"People should not be alarmed by prankster spirits. If you were in a room, and you were invisible, you too would want to be noticed."

n 1871, Walter Montgomery was a carefree ten-year-old boy living on Boulder's west Pearl Street when he went to visit his father at a nearby mining camp. It was a short trip from which, sadly, Walter never returned. Or so it seemed at the time.

Anthony Arnett, a prominent Boulder pioneer, built the Pearl Street house. Arnett arrived in Colorado in 1859 and was involved in mining, freighting, and hotel operation. After moving to Boulder, Arnett ran the Arnett Hotel and was involved in the construction of the Black Hawk-Central City and Caribou-Central City wagon roads. He owned several mines in Boulder County and donated land for the university. In 1896, Benjamin F. Montgomery, who took part in the famous Sand Creek Massacre, bought the property.

Montgomery was also involved in Boulder's early mining operations and was in the mountains working when he sent for his young son. After arriving, Walter suddenly became ill and died a few days later. Walter's sister, Frances Montgomery Hoover, in her book, *Castle o' Montgomery*, describes seeing him healthy for the last time.

"While Mother packed his clothes I went in search of him. I found him down by the creek, fishing. We hustled him off. I remember his little white face at the car window, our last words of caution and advice, the quick nervous flutter of his hand waving to us as the train pulled out."

Walter's motivation for haunting his boyhood home seems to be a desire to return to his happy life there, where he could play with his brother and sisters and go fishing. After all, Walter's house is nothing like those typically depicted in haunted house stories. The blue Victorian is immaculate and surrounded by small shops on Pearl Street selling flowers, antiques, and pastries.

There aren't many people who have spent time at the Montgomery House on Pearl Street, now an office complex with an upstairs apartment, who don't have stories about Walter. They may not know his name, but they soon learn that he's like many precocious boys—he demands a lot of attention.

Initially, officer workers wanted to blame the age of the house for unexplained and mysterious electrical problems. The frame house was built well before the turn of the 19th century. It's a prominent visual landmark. The house is made of clapboard to the second floor, with fancy shingles to the eaves. Portico pediment repeats at the roofline and features decorative wood trim.

Nate Tiens and his co-workers rented office space in the

16

house and were so enamored with Walter's spirit, they were eager to talk to local reporters for the annual Halloween newspaper article. Tiens described buying Walter a little red wagon and a basketball so he'd have something to play with other than the light switches that were forever being turned off and on. "I was working late, and the lights kept flickering," said Tiens. "I had to get a project done, and finally I called out: 'Walter, stop it!' The light stayed on and couldn't be shut off for the next twelve hours."

Boulder psychic Krista Socash says Tiens did the right thing. "People should not be alarmed by prankster spirits. If you were in a room, and you were invisible, you too would want to be noticed. They just want acknowledgment. Just try talking to them. Ask them to leave if you are uncomfortable."

His fellow employees laughed when Tiens first claimed that a ghost was responsible for the lights turning on and off in their offices, but they were eventually convinced because there was no other logical explanation. "It couldn't have been electrical because the computers were on, and they were all plugged into the same power source," says co-worker Mark Lyten. At one point, an entourage of Russian politicians visited the office on a tour of small Boulder businesses. "We were telling the Russian women about the ghost, and it started happening again," says Lyten. "It was kind of annoying because we needed the lights to show them what we do. But that is what made us all believe."

Briggs Geister rented an upstairs apartment at the Montgomery House. She hadn't even settled in when Walter made his first appearance. "The first time I took a shower I looked out through the shower door and saw something blue. I thought 'What on earth did I leave out there that was blue?' I opened the door and nothing was there, and when I closed the door the blue was gone."

Unnerved, Geister eventually accepted the feeling that she was being watched or that a "presence" was near. "I felt it and my two cats often behaved like there was something there. Their heads would turn, as though they were watching something. They weren't afraid of it, but they seemed to be watching something that wasn't there."

Over the years, Walter has been called mildly annoying and Geister soon learned why. She was constantly losing things. "Knowing I had set it there, I'd go back and it wouldn't be there. I'd have to search and search." The items were usually just moved to a new location and the hide-and-seek game typically only occurred when Geister was cleaning house.

Like the office workers who encountered Walter, Geister soon discovered his fascination with the plumbing. "In the middle of the night the toilet in the downstairs office space would flush. And there would be nobody down there."

Geister never saw Walter while she was living at the Montgomery House and has mixed feelings about it. "In some ways I wish I had seen him, but in other ways I'm glad I didn't." Geister says she felt protected by Walter—that he was a "good little spirit."

"A young boy with a fondness for pranks." That's how psychic Hope Hewetson described Walter during a 1999 Halloween Spirit Tour sponsored by Historic Boulder. Without any information about the house's history, Hewetson relayed her impressions of Walter to those participating in the annual fundraiser. Hewetson said the young boy was a strong presence in the house. "It was clear that he had an untimely death and the house was where his sense of family remained. He wanted to play and seemed to be delighted that the adults were confused as to the goings-on in the house. He was tickled when people said things like, 'Little Walter is at it again.'"

But the Montgomery house is old and Walter may not be alone. That would perhaps explain Nate Tiens' more frightening experiences. The longer he kept the office space at the Montgomery House, the more uncomfortable it became.

"The reason we moved the business from the Montgomery House was partially because of Walter—to get away from the little guy both physically and mentally. I had some good and some really bad experiences there. My experiences on the bad side were really bad," says Tiens. "They involved the subconscious, the dark side, actually evil."

Geister doesn't argue. She relates most of her ghostly encounters as amusing but says on two occasions she was terrorized by "something else." "One time a friend was over and we were having tea in the apartment. We were suddenly overcome by a horrible sensation." They didn't relate the feeling to Walter, but another presence. "We were terrified. I've never been so scared in my life. We were so scared, we began talking to Walter, 'Walter! Get this thing out of here—whatever it is!'"

When it happened a second time, Geister said she knew it wasn't Walter. "It didn't feel like it was a someone—more like a *something*—like it came from somewhere else. Knowing Walter was there was somehow a comfort."

Psychic Hewetson is not surprised that Walter's spirit would provide consolation. "I got the sense that Walter has been ready, or able to leave—to have a reincarnation process for quite some time. But he just doesn't really care that he could come back. Things are fine with him just as they are."

Apparently so. A design firm is one of several businesses that currently occupies office space in the house. According to an employee, design materials are kept in a variety of wicker baskets on various desks. A former employee working at night told her colleagues that the baskets repeatedly moved on their own accord, and were constantly being rearranged. "Now no one wants to work there at night," says one of the designers. "It's a lovely old house and a great work space, but it's like someone is always playing a practical joke on everyone else."

The Montgomery House is one of Boulder's earliest remaining residences, and home to one of its oldest ghosts—a little boy, who watches from a basement window, fiddles with the lights and is forever intrigued by modern plumbing. ❖

What is a ghost? A tragedy condemned to repeat itself
time and again? An instant of pain, perhaps.
Something dead which still seems to be alive.
An emotion suspended in time.
Like a blurred photograph.
Like an insect trapped in amber.

———————————

"El Espinazo del Diablo"

THE DECKER—TYLER HOUSE

Chapter 1

THE DECKER-TYLER HOUSE

It's as though the house is still waiting for Captain Tyler's return.

I n 1987, when Kathryn Howes, a transplanted preservation architect from Washington, D.C., first set foot in the Decker-Tyler House in north Boulder, she knew that she had to have it. Despite the home's disrepair, and the look of disbelief on her husband's face, she knew that she belonged in the house. She knew it was meant to be hers and that her family was destined to restore the house to its former glory. Since that first day, Kathryn has felt a strong connection to the Gothic Revival farmhouse that was once the home of Clinton M. Tyler and his family. She has also felt the presence of spirits who seem to watch over her.

During Halloween week in 1999, as part of Historic Boulder's Spirit Tour, visitors were treated to a tour of the home led by a psychic from Psychic Horizons. A gentle breeze rustled the branches of the redbud tree, the oldest in

23

Boulder, that arches over the walkway. The lights in the jack-o-lanterns flickered, making the pumpkins with their wicked smiles seem to laugh at those who passed by. The visitors were in for a treat as they learned about the spirits that roam the house, so beautifully restored by Kathryn and her husband.

Built in 1874, the Decker-Tyler House sat on eighty-three acres of prime farmland which Clinton Tyler bought from Judge J. H. Decker. Early photographs show the home as the only structure standing for miles in north Boulder. Architect E. H. Dimick, who designed the University of Colorado's Old Main, also designed the Tyler home which now stands out as the only historic building in a sea of '50s ranch houses. As one of Boulder's earliest pioneers, Clinton Tyler had great foresight for the opportunities the area had to offer. Known as a generous and highly energetic man, he was one of the city's wealthiest citizens with interests in livestock, agriculture, construction, sawmills, real estate, and even politics. At the time of his death, his holdings reportedly included over 13,000 acres of land throughout seven Colorado counties including 1,000 acres in Boulder. His financial interests extended to the territory of Wyoming as well.

In 1860, Tyler came to Boulder from Wisconsin with his wife Sarah, their son, and Tyler's father-in-law and family. They originally settled in Black Hawk, drawn to the area by the promise of gold. There he ran a six-stamp quartz mill, the first of its kind in the state, brought by wagon on his journey from the Midwest. Designed with large cylinders that crushed the ore, some stamp mills of the time were very transportable and Tyler's was one of the largest in the area. He ran his own custom mill and this income formed the base of what would become a vast fortune.

In addition to his milling interests, Tyler was also known in the area as a patriot. During the 1864 Indian scare, he was the first man to answer the call for volunteers to protect citizens from Indian raids and was commissioned by Colorado Governor John Evans as the captain of a Third Cavalry unit. Called the "100 Days Men," and "The Rough and Ready Tyler Rangers," the group provided protection normally supplied by the Army. With the soldiers away fighting the Civil War, the Indians had greater opportunity to reclaim their tribal lands and uproot the miners and other settlers. Not only did Tyler ride with the unit, he also furnished many of the horses ridden by the men.

Tyler is also credited with the construction of Boulder Canyon's first toll road, linking Boulder to the mining communities of Central City and Black Hawk. This was a major undertaking given the geography of the canyon. Toll was collected at two stations on either end of the road. One dollar was charged for each wagon and train; seventy-five cents for carriages. No toll was collected if travelers were on the road to attend a funeral or church services.

In 1872, the family settled in Boulder and Tyler quickly established himself as a well-respected citizen. Tyler's connections with the University of Colorado are legendary. Local historians say that on a blustery winter night in January of 1875, a weary rider approached the Tyler home. The Hon. D. H. Nichols had come from a meeting of the Territorial Legislature on most urgent business. Several Colorado towns were being considered for public institutions. If Tyler would promise the initial funds of $15,000, "an institution of higher learning" would be awarded to Boulder.

Tyler pledged his support, gave the rider a fresh horse, and sent him on his way. And the rest, as they say, is history.

In 1884, Tyler was appointed a regent of the University of Colorado. His family, which grew to include five sons and three daughters, continued its ties with the university. His daughter Ella was the first woman to graduate from the school in 1886, and her husband, prominent Boulder lawyer Richard Whitely, was in the school's first graduating class, in 1882, consisting of only six men. Tyler's son Bert was also a student at the university when he died of meningitis at the age of twenty-one.

Tyler, astride his big bay gelding, was a familiar sight in Boulder and the surrounding towns. He was frequently away for days on end while his family waited for his safe return. The house was built with an Indian tunnel, a long underground tunnel leading to an outer structure, which would allow the family to escape in the event of an Indian attack. The entrance to the tunnel is still located in the cellar of the home, but has never been explored by Kathryn or her family.

Whether he had ridden off to attend to business or fight the Indian wars in the late 1800s, it's as though the house still waits for Tyler's return. The spirit of a woman, possibly his wife, waits at the top of the main staircase. She is one of the most prevalent energies in the home and Kathryn has often felt her friendly presence. Whether it is a change in air temperature or currents, she senses an almost nurturing feeling that seems at times to come out of nowhere.

Psychic Krista Socash visited the home before the night of the Historic Boulder Spirit Tour to do an interpretation of the house. She went without any prior knowledge of its history or what Kathryn had been sensing. She too felt the woman on the stairs. "She is very happy that Kathryn owns this home," Krista says. "She is very pleased that Kathryn is here."

Immediately upon entering the house, Krista turned around towards the front door through which she had just entered, and saw the apparition of a big bay horse staring back at her through the screen. "I felt the very strong presence of a big horse that seemed very loyal to its owner." At this, Kathryn was eager for her to see a historic picture of the home, framed and hanging in the kitchen. It was an old photograph of the house which included three of the family's horses standing outside near the front door. "These must be the horses you are seeing," she said pointing to the photograph. But Krista pointed out another horse in the photo, a large bay standing to the right of the others. Kathryn was surprised. "I had lived in the house with that photo on the wall for twelve years," she said, "and I had never seen that horse in the photograph."

Krista's visit brought other presences to light that Kathryn had long suspected inhabited the home. The energies of two young girls playing in the upstairs hallway were very prevalent, perhaps the spirits of the Tyler daughters. During the Historic Boulder Spirit Tour, Kathryn and Krista said that a young boy pulled away from his parents and apparently wandered up the stairs. In the middle of Krista's discussion about the home, the boy returned and asked in a frightened voice who the two young girls were that he had seen playing in the upstairs hallway. He had actually seen the spirits, as many young children can.

Krista was also drawn to one particular room in the home

from which several strong presences emanated. What is now an extra upstairs bedroom felt to Krista like it had been used as a healing room, or a room where sick people in the Tyler family had gone to recover. In those days, many children shared a room and didn't have the luxury of spending time in a hospital when they were ill, or taking medication for a speedy recovery as they might today. Therefore, some homes had an area or a room where those who were ill could be separated from the rest of the family to recuperate. Surprised by what Krista sensed, Kathryn mentioned that ever since they had moved in, she and her husband had called that room the healing room and had slept there whenever they felt ill. Ironically, they too had sensed the room's therapeutic spirits. Krista also felt the energies of a sick young boy in the room, and an older woman who sat looking out at the lights of Boulder through the window. She also said that a feeling of death, one that felt like a miscarriage, was prevalent in the room.

When another psychic visited the home with Krista he revealed another spirit. Upon entering what is now the dining room, he immediately pointed to a corner where a large armoire sits. "I feel the energy of an unhappy black man in the corner and I see something having to do with water." Unable to make sense of the feeling, he and Kathryn looked at the home's original blueprints. To their surprise, the blueprints showed that the corner had once been the location of the sink in the original kitchen. Interestingly enough, the 1885 Census Report lists one household domestic living at the home.

Perhaps the most intriguing part of this story is the research Kathryn has done which may hold the key to the strong attraction she feels to her home. The actual geographical paths of western migration of both her grandmother's family and the family of Clinton Tyler were very close, down to the same town in one instance. Kathryn's research on her family shows that her grandmother on her father's side was a Tyler and supposedly a distant relative of the tenth president, John Tyler. Her grandmother's family came from New York and New Hampshire, eventually settling in Clinton, Iowa. Clinton Tyler's family traveled from the East to Wisconsin where the rest of Kathryn's relatives lived, then settled in Clinton, Iowa before their journey westward. Is Kathryn a relative of the Clinton Tyler family? Has she come full-circle to own a home that unbeknownst to her was once inhabited by her own relatives? The woman on the stairs seems to think so. ❖

THE ORIGINAL HAUNTED HOUSE

Chapter 5

THE ORIGINAL HAUNTED HOUSE

When the dogs died they were treated to expensive funerals, complete with caskets, hearses, and headstones.

A sk Boulder's older citizens, those who grew up here in the early 1900s, and they'll all tell you the same thing: the Harbeck House is the city's original haunted house. Stories of strange lights and ghostly figures in the windows were the fodder for what became an urban legend of sorts. Everyone knew the house *must* be haunted...it's the Harbeck House.

Sitting at the corner of 12th and Euclid, the house is a grand sight indeed. Built in 1899 by J.H. Harbeck as a summer home, the house was known for its unique architectural style. Indiana limestone, Grecian ionic columns, and a nine-foot-high Tiffany stained-glass window add to its charm. Harbeck and his wife, Kate, lived in New York City where he worked as a stockbroker and owned a thriving dry-goods chain. Historical records report that he also owned the glorious Plaza Hotel.

Summering in Colorado proved to be beneficial to John's health and though they socialized with a small group of friends when visiting, they remained somewhat to themselves. This is where some of the strange tales of the Harbeck House originate.

Katherine's fear of illness prompted her to be seen in public with her face covered, often wearing a dark veil. The Harbecks traveled about town in an elaborate carriage with the curtains drawn. The couple's love of their three dogs, Beauty, Jim, and Rover, would become a legend of its own. Childless, the dogs were their "children" and they were regarded as members of the family. When the dogs died they were treated to expensive funerals, complete with caskets, hearses, and headstones. The dogs were buried in a plot in Katherine's garden on the southwest side of the home.

John died in 1910 in New York City, leaving Katherine with the Boulder home. Unwilling to sell it because her beloved pets were still buried on the grounds, she hired a caretaker to watch over the empty house and care for the graves. According to DeAnne Butterfield, executive director of the Boulder History Museum, the caretaker apparently had a vivid imagination and told the local children ghost stories to keep them at bay while the house remained unoccupied. But the stories took on a life of their own. The local children believed it was haunted and would not be convinced otherwise. Those children, now grown old, still believe it is haunted.

For years the house and the dog's graves stood unharmed. Kate Harbeck died in 1931 when she was tragically crushed in a revolving door at the Plaza Hotel, her New

York City home. She had never returned to Colorado since the death of her husband and the dining room table in her Boulder home was still set for a dinner party that was never held.

Kate Harbeck died a very wealthy woman and her generous will bequeathed $50,000 to the Society for the Prevention of Cruelty to Animals, a local chapter which eventually became the Boulder Humane Society. It was her wish that the remains of the dogs be re-interred at a pet cemetery, located at the time in a field on Arapahoe Ave. It is believed that the dogs are still buried in the property's tall grass, well away from the bustling city life that surrounds them.

The Harbeck House stood empty for nearly thirty years before it became home to several families. In 1937, the land surrounding the house was purchased by William Beach and became what is now known as Beach Park. The Bergheim family lived in the house for thirty years. Milton Bergheim owned and operated a clothing store on Pearl Street. The Bergheim children were a lively bunch and turned one of the upstairs rooms into a rollerskating rink. The house became a place of activity and family gatherings, quite a change from its days of drawn curtains and locked doors.

Since becoming the home of the Boulder History Museum in 1985, the ghost stories have slowly faded away. Employees and volunteers at the museum have heard the house is haunted but none have ever experienced anything out of the ordinary.

But maybe we shouldn't be so quick to dismiss the ghostly activity. On a recent visit to the house, psychic Brian Hall felt the presence of a woman watching over the home. "I sensed that this was her house and she was very protective of it," he says. "She is still there watching over it and guarding it." Hall felt her spirit standing at the window of what was once a bedroom on the top floor looking out over the garden.

Do ghosts still roam the halls of the Harbeck House? Ask around. You'll be surprised at what you hear. ❖

While yet a boy I sought for ghosts, and sped
Through many a listening chamber, cave and ruin,
And starlight wood, with fearful steps pursuing
Hopes of high talks with the departed dead.
I called on poisonous names with which our youth is fed.

_____

"Hymn to Intellectual Beauty"
Percy Bysshe Shelley

35

Photo by Ann Alexander Leggett

EERIE HAPPENINGS AT BERKELEY FARM

Chapter 6

EERIE HAPPENINGS AT BERKELEY FARM

"My mother would only say, 'Just leave them alone, they won't hurt you.'"

t's hard to doubt claims that spirits regularly visit Boulder's historic Berkeley Farm. Sitting at a picnic table near the White Rock Ditch that runs through the property, there's no denying the eerie atmosphere. The ancient canopy of trees invokes a heavy, solemn sensation combined with a dizzy light-headedness. There is incredible beauty here, but also a palpable sense of anger, joy, disappointment, hard labor, success, and death. If ghost stories are to be believed, the strongest feeling is a desire to be remembered.

"One spirit present is Junius Berkeley," says property owner Diana Linnen. "Until I had a plaque installed outside of Old Main on the CU campus acknowledging his contributions to the community, you could constantly hear men bickering under a tree near the house. I heard it, my renters heard it, and psychics heard it. He played a huge role in the establishment of this property but the history books forgot him. He wants to know why."

In 2003, the Berkeley Farm will have been in Diana's family for 140 years. It's the sixth oldest original territorial property in Colorado and has been continuously owned by the same family. Hidden from the street by tall trees and bushes, visitors travel down a winding gravel driveway to a grouping of 19th century buildings. In 1863, this was a property of 320 acres in what was considered "east" Boulder. The small acreage on Walnut is all that is left of the original homestead. The property has four structures: two rental houses, the original brick "cook house," and a barn that dates from 1880.

There are two generations of Berkeley men who left their mark on Boulder. Judge Granville Berkeley, Sr., and his sons Junius Berkeley, and Granville Berkeley, Jr. Psychics who have visited the property say it has a very male energy, hard working and serious. But the men are not the only spirits who remain at the farm.

According to Diana, Clarissa Cordelia Berkeley said before she died that she would return in the spring, with the violets. "'If there are violets in the grass, then I am here,' is what she told my mother and grandmother." In certain years the lawn at Berkeley Farm is covered in clumps of delicate violets, while other years there are none.

The Berkeley legacy is a long one. Junius Berkeley was the first of the pioneering family to arrive in Boulder from Virginia. An original piece of flagstone with his initials and the date, June 1, 1862 is still on the property. His father and brother followed in 1863. Berkeley, Sr., known as the "Ditch Digger" of Boulder, incorporated the Boulder Valley Railroad and White Rock Ditch Company. In 1863, along with his wife

Anna, he homesteaded the 320 acres in downtown Boulder and in 1874 plotted what was called "Block D. East Boulder."

The Berkeleys were strong advocates of the movement to establish a university in Boulder and offered land for the institution. In the late 1870s, Granville Berkeley, Sr., by then Judge Berkeley, was the first president of the Board of Trustees of the University of Colorado. He is remembered for his florid speeches and according to Phyllis Smith's book, *A Look at Boulder*, made some prophetic predictions in 1869.

That year, some 1,500 people were visiting Boulder County's first fair and Judge Granville had been asked to make one of his famous speeches. He predicted that the Boulder Valley would soon support "railways, telegraphs, academies, manufactories, and other appliances of civilization." He also exhorted the ladies to "cultivate flowers and small fruits to make homes attractive to their male relatives, and thus win them from the ways of temptation."

According to F.O. Repplier in *As A Town Grows*, Granville Berkeley, Sr. was also one of the earliest members of the new school board, elected in 1867 when Boulder had a population of about 325 people.

Continuing in his father's footsteps, Junius Berkeley was the first secretary of the Board of Regents of the University of Colorado, a position he held for two terms. The younger son, Granville Berkeley, Jr., was one of Boulder's pioneer lawyers and among the first to harvest ice in Boulder. He built the Citizen's National Bank building, which at one time bore the family name. He was also the foreman for the first volunteer fire department in Boulder and served with the Colorado Volunteers at Sand Creek. It was this Berkeley that married Clarissa Cordelia.

Harvesting ice is a lost art, but in 1863 it was a booming business. Natural ice cut from Berkeley Lake was stored in what is now the main rental house on the Berkeley Farm, and was sold to the community. Most of the unexplained ghostly activity has been reported in or around this "Ice House." Although it looks quaint from the outside, things have happened in the house that don't fit that description.

"There's a closet off the kitchen and when I was a girl it had a curtain in front of it," says Diana. "The curtain would suddenly move, just start blowing back and forth. I repeatedly asked my mother what was going on but she would only say, 'Just leave them alone. They won't hurt you.'"

Diana says that's not all that moves. "The furniture moves. Dressers and beds move. Once after returning with my aunt from a trip to California, we walked in and the rocking chair was rocking. In disbelief we walked over to take a closer look and on the fireplace mantel next to the rocking chair there was an ancient calling card that read, "Granville Berkeley, Jr." To this day, I can't tell you how it got there. When she was alive, my aunt wouldn't stay at the house. She would stay at a hotel rather than stay there. We didn't really talk about it but then she didn't have to explain it to me."

According to Diana's husband, Larry Linnen, several tenants have also been spooked by activities at what was the Ice House. "Once we rented the house to the sister of a rather well-known professional football player. It took her a week to move in. Within three days she called and said she couldn't live there, that it wasn't right for her. She moved everything out in one day. We didn't even charge her anything because we were pretty sure the spirits had frightened her off. We didn't ask for any details as to why she couldn't stay. We knew why."

When Diana married Larry she remained quiet about her experiences with spirits at the farm. She admits to being afraid she'd scare him off—that he'd think she was a little too wacky. The spirits, however, haven't been so considerate to Larry.

"There's a lot to be done, keeping up the property, the two rental houses and outbuildings, so we sometimes spend the night," he says. "One night, Diana was staying at the small house with a friend who was recuperating from surgery so I stayed at the Ice House. I was asleep in an upstairs bedroom when I suddenly woke up—I was instantly awake. The air around me was heavy and I didn't have any idea why. I was uncomfortable, so I thought I'd distract myself by watching television for awhile. I went downstairs to the living room and while I was watching TV the heaviness of the air disappeared. About thirty seconds later the dog that belonged to the woman recuperating at the other house suddenly began barking madly. That was unusual because the dog rarely, if ever, barked. It wasn't until these unexplained events had happened to me on several occasions that I put it together. Now I believe the spirit, or ghost, or presence, whatever you want to call it, had left me and was in the yard. That's what caused the dog to bark.

"A second time, I was sleeping overnight and I was again instantly awakened from a sound sleep. Next to me on the floor was a mirror lying face-up that, until then, had been hanging on the wall. I thought it must have been the mirror hitting the floor that woke me up. But the odd thing was, the mirror had been on the opposite wall next to the bed, which means it had to fall to the floor, over me, and over the bed. It

41

wasn't broken, but instead appeared to have been placed on the floor next to the bed.

"Another time it was midday and I tried to take a nap between the chores I was doing. Suddenly something kicked the underside of the bed and woke me up. I figured the spirits didn't like the fact that I was resting. They wanted me to get the chores done. A nap would not have been part of their work ethic and they didn't think it should be part of mine."

During Historic Boulder's Spirit Tour in 2000, psychic Krista Socash said a man on a horse was watching them from near the old barn. "This was a proud, stubborn, hard-drinking man with a Wild West attitude," says Socash. "The area was a neighborhood hang-out of sorts." Socash also sensed that slavery had been in the property's history and she was not far from the truth.

"When the family came west, the black family that had worked for them in Virginia came along," says Linnen. The psychic claimed that all was not well between the Berkeleys and their servants, but Linnen says there's no proof they were mistreated. "They were servants, and they were likely treated like most servants in those days."

For many years, the senior Granville lived at 1846 22nd Street. The smaller of the two rental houses at Berkeley Farm was then the cook's house, and Judge Granville's meals were prepared there and delivered to his house on 22nd Street by wagon. Following his death in 1884, the family suffered a reversal of fortunes, forcing Granville Berkeley, Jr. to move his family into the Ice House in the early 1890s.

This was no doubt devastating for such a proud man and may explain why the psychic felt there had been much unhappiness on the property at one time. Despite today's appearances, it was an isolated and lonely spot in the 1890s. Granville, Jr. lived another forty-seven years after his father's death and had plenty of time to ruminate about what "might have been."

Junius Berkeley would have had his own complaints. He was set to inherit the Berkeley Farm, but he died in 1907 at the age of sixty-five, twenty-four years before Granville Berkeley, Jr. passed away in 1931 at the age of eighty-five. In addition, Junius is rarely mentioned in history books. Linnen wanted to install plaques at the university and around the Berkeley property so each man would be acknowledged for his contributions to the city and state. In part, she also wanted to ease some of the ill-will she senses on the property. "I have to say I believe I've appeased the men, to some extent," says Linnen.

Diana believes one of the female energies may also have had a hand in getting the family name recognized. Lydia Berkeley was Judge Granville's second wife after the death of Anna. Linnen believes she's probably still there because she too is determined to have the family name remembered.

"The trouble is, the spirits don't just haunt me when I'm on the farm," says Diana. "They latch onto me. I don't find them, they find me. I've had similar experiences in my home in Denver with objects floating, and also being kicked from under the bed. When you realize the energy it must take to come back and touch base with the living, it makes me want to figure out what they're trying to tell me."

OK. If not Clarissa Cordelia, maybe it's Lydia that the current tenant has seen walking across the yard. In an attempt to reach Diana to research this book, the tenant was called, and in the course of conversation told about the *Haunted Boulder* book and the plan to include a chapter about the Berkeley Farm. She had moved to Boulder from New York only thirty days before and knew nothing about the property's history. Without hesitation she burst out, "I've seen her. More than once I've seen a woman walking in the yard. She appears to be dressed in a cape, but I can't make out her face. In fact, it's almost like she doesn't have a head."

Or maybe it's neither Lydia nor Clarissa. In the early part of the century, Linnen's grandmother and her seven-year-old daughter came for a visit. Exact details are not remembered, but the girl either fell from an overhead tree or was walking on top of a picket fence near the first cook's house when she slipped. A stake from the fence pieced her throat and she died almost instantly. Would that explain the headless woman?

Whatever the tenant saw, it was so upsetting that she called a healer, an energy worker to help rid her of the disturbing visions.

Linnen wants nothing to do with that approach to the ghosts on her property. "I don't want them to leave," says Diana. "Despite what I've seen, or felt, or been disturbed by, I don't have any plans to exorcise the property. I feel respectful about who is there. The bottom line is, I don't want anyone trying to get rid of my ghosts." ❖

Clarissa Cordelia Berkeley

Photo by Ann Alexander Leggett

THE CASTLE HOUSE

Chapter 7

THE CASTLE HOUSE

"We traced the sound of the old-time music to an empty corner in the basement, but there was no radio there, just old-time music coming from nowhere."

I f there's a house in Boulder that looks like it ought to be haunted, it's the Castle House on Ninth Street.

Angled at a slant on the corner lot, the distinctive vine-covered house with octagonal towers on either side is impossible to miss, especially with the two gargoyles keeping vigil on the roof. In other words, the Castle has all the makings for a spine-tingling haunted house story even before the front door has opened. And who knows what stories the front door might tell?

Made of red brick and white stone, the house stands on University Hill in the shadow of the Flatirons. The beautiful home, built in 1905, features octagonal walls, parapets, and high windows. Legend has it that a beautiful young woman promised to marry whichever of two suitors built her the most unusual house. According to the story, she married the gentleman who built the Castle House.

That man was Benjamin Franklin Gregg, a brick mason by trade. A woman to woo or not, Gregg was a stickler for detail. The house is notable for its asymmetrical composition. The arcaded porch has bands of brick decorating the arches. A lover's balcony above the porch roof features chiseled brick walls with stone trim. Local historians consider the house a neighborhood landmark, because it's an unusual example of the Tudor style in Boulder.

Aagghh…if it were just that simple.

"The house is obsessive," says Ruth Savig. "When I saw it, it was love at first sight. I had to have it. I loved it. But it was an ominous house."

Savig and her family owned the house for about ten years and lived in it for four. She tells of unexplained visions, sounds, and odors in the house. "I don't know if it's ghosts or not, but there sure as hell is something in there." Savig admits she's always had an affinity with the "other side" but says that doesn't explain the events experienced by her two children.

"One night, my young daughter came running into our bedroom. She said, 'Mommy, there's a big man who keeps shaking my bed.' I asked her if she could have been dreaming. She said, 'No, he woke me up and won't let me go back to sleep.'" The heavy brass bed that came with the house had been moved away from the wall. "Not much, but it had been moved and there's no way my four-year-old daughter could have moved it." Savig was later told that the previous owner's father had died in that bedroom, and he was a big man, standing well above six feet. A psychic told Savig she had bad feelings about the room and that no one should sleep in it because there is a "very angry old man there." The Savigs moved their daughter to another bedroom.

"My son and I were alone in the house once when we heard 1920s music that sounded like it was coming from a tinny old radio. No radios were on in the house and we didn't have a TV set. We traced the sound of the old-time music to an empty corner of the basement, but there was no radio there, just old-time music coming from nowhere. Later, a friend told me that sometimes sounds get caught in a space. It's like physics tells us, nothing is ever lost…if there's a better explanation, I'd like to hear it.

"There were only four of us in the house, myself, my husband, and the two children but the house always felt crowded. It always felt to me as though large groups of people were standing around."

If a house needed to accommodate a crowd, the Castle House certainly could have obliged. When it was built, it had twenty-three rooms on five levels—a basement, servant's quarters, the main floor, a mezzanine, and the top floor. An unusually wide front door may have been more than just an aesthetic touch. "There's speculation the house may have been a funeral parlor or mortuary," says Savig. "That means they would have had to bring caskets through the front door."

Historic Boulder asked local psychic Jenny Scharf for her impressions of the house during the 1999 Historic Boulder Spirit Tour. Scharf had never met Savig, but confirmed her beliefs.

"At the homeowner's request, I didn't have access to the entire house but I could tell there was a very large man there working in the basement or in a garage-like area," says

Scharf. "I couldn't say for sure that he was an undertaker, only that he worked with dead bodies. He had a very scientific approach. He didn't view his work as morbid as others might, just very interesting. He enjoyed the experimentation process."

But which undertaker would that be? According to historical records from Boulder's Carnegie Library, not just one, but two morticians lived at the Castle House. In 1985, Lorraine "Kelly" Kelso Jacobson told an interviewer with Boulder's Oral History Program that her father, Edward Kelso, noted as a "pioneer" Boulder mortician, bought the house in 1932 while she was still in high school. Until that time, the house was occupied by the second owner, Edward Fair, a mortician from Iowa who settled in Boulder in 1918. Did they take their work home with them? Is one of them still perfecting the flawless corpse? Because certainly there would have been enough space for such work, especially in the "dungeon."

"Every castle has to have a dungeon—and that's the dungeon," Jane Fitz Randolph told historian Jane Valentine Barker when interviewed for Barker's book, *76 Boulder Historic Houses*. The fourth owner of the Castle House, Fitz Randolph describes in detail all the dazzling public rooms, but also refers to the funny room under the front porch, "the low-ceilinged, dirt-floor storage area"—the dungeon—is what she called it.

If Fitz Randolph experienced ghosts at the Castle House, she never said. But while Savig lived there she repeatedly brought people in to "cleanse" the house. "Things got so wild, I brought someone over to bless the house, but they just couldn't do it in one whack. Every psychic I brought in felt something. The house was full of energy.

"Nobody would stay in the parlor for very long. It was always cold and people would go in there for about five minutes and then had to get out. Later, a psychic told me the room had several spirits trapped there—there were multiple personalities afoot.

"I would walk through the house sometimes and smell spring flowers when there were none in the house. Various perfumes were regularly wafting through the house. But the strangest odor I remember was when my father was ill. I hadn't been told he was ill and he was hundreds of miles away, but I smelled the warm milk you smell when cows are being milked." The smell of warm milk? Savig's father was a dairy farmer.

Now a well-known artist in Greeley, Colorado, Savig describes the original architecture of the house as very masculine. Still, she had more experiences with female energy than male energy.

"I was sitting in the dining room late one night when I was suddenly aware of a lot of animosity in the room. I saw an old woman sitting across the room. I didn't really 'see' her, I guess it was sort of with my mind's eye. I drew her picture on a piece of paper. I could hear her saying to me. 'This is my house! I don't want you or your husband or your children in my house!'" Savig said she shouted back at the woman and told her to leave.

Psychic Scharf believes the woman is still there because she's waiting for someone. "When I visited, the female energy was on the first landing of the stairs that go to the second floor. I sensed that there might have been a piano on the landing during her time at the house. In any case, she spent a lot of time there waiting, playing the piano, and waiting. She seemed to be expecting her suitor, but ironically he was sitting in the swing on the front porch. They were both unaware of each other's presence."

In 1968, the Savigs moved to Greeley, but continued to own the house for several more years. They sold it in 1975.

"I sometimes think *people* are haunted, not houses. But I still believe it was the house itself and not some predisposition on my part, that brought things on." And if Savig's encounters with spirits were based on her own desire to believe in the paranormal, what then explains what the next owner experienced—the one after Ruth Savig?

"I saw a woman hanging in midair, dressed in pre-turn of the century (fashions). She was standing by the window outfitted in a cloak. She was just looking at me, and then she went away. I've nonetheless always had a feeling of welcome in this house, like no harm would come to me or mine." It's the only ghost encounter an owner since Savig has related, but surely it's not the last.

Although it's been more than thirty years since Ruth Savig lived in the Castle House, she recounts her experiences as though it was yesterday. "It was a beautiful and interesting house and I loved it. Some of the happiest and most miserable times of my life were spent at the Castle. I hated to let it go even after what had happened to me. But there's something terrifying about that house."

Terrifying perhaps, but the Castle House remains one of Boulder's most beloved landmarks. ❖

Now is the time of night
That graves, all gaping wide,
Everyone lets forth his sprite
In the church-way paths to glide.

———————————

"A Midsummer Night's Dream"
William Shakespeare

Photo by Ann Alexander Leggett

THE MINER'S HOUSE ON MAPLETON

Chapter 8

THE MINER'S HOUSE ON MAPLETON

When she got to the part about the man living a very simple life, the front porch light flickered and went out once again.

The spirits in some houses are not as active as in others, yet at the same time their presence can be very profound. This is certainly the case with the Darnall House on Mapleton. When the front door of this old home opens, a trip through time begins. It's a journey back to the Victorian era complete with a front parlor, rich wallcoverings, and heavy, red velvet draperies. Diana Darnall and her husband have made only subtle changes to the house since they purchased it in 1995. Their goal was simple: make the home comfortable and livable while maintaining its rich historic character. The end result is a stunning mixture of beauty and Victorian charm.

The history of the house and its residents is colorful indeed. Built in 1874, the house sits on land which was originally part of a larger tract given as bounty land, land granted to military personnel in payment for their services to the United States Army. The original tract, some 160 acres, was given by the General Land Office to Demetrio Arnuncito in 1866. He was a volunteer soldier who was a tracker with the New Mexican Volunteers in the Navajo Indian wars. The land remained one large parcel until 1873, when the North Boulder Addition was created. Several changes in ownership took place over the next few years. Mary S. Scott purchased the property from Asbury Staples on June 12, 1875, and remained the owner until her death in 1900 at age sixty-five. Based on title transfer records and *Boulder County News* clips from 1874, it seems apparent that Mr. Staples built the house that remains on the site today, although at that time Mapleton Avenue was known as Hill Street.

Well-respected citizens Mary Scott and her husband, Holland, operated a grocery and confectionery store on Pearl Street. Holland was also the manager of McAllister Supply and Lumber at the corner of 15th and Pearl Streets in Boulder. A *Daily Camera* obituary reports that Mary died in the house on June 21, 1900.

In 1918, Mr. Otis Pearl Pherson moved into the home with his wife Ida, who worked as a sales clerk in Boulder until she retired. Otis was a colorful character who mined gold, silver, and tungsten. Bud Chesebro, born in Boulder in 1919, worked for Otis Pherson when Pherson managed the Grand Republic Mine in Salida. Chesebro thought his boss was a fine fellow. "He expected an honest day's work from you, which was common in those days, but he was a good man to work for. He was one of those people who had no enemies."

For over sixty years, the Phersons lived in the house, and Otis, growing older, began to write of his long, interesting life. Locals report that he had a fascination with electricity and he would expound on his theories to whomever would listen. He was also very interested in ghosts and told stories about Boulder's haunted locations. Well known for the many colorful and pointed letters he wrote to the editor of the *Daily Camera*, a sometimes cantankerous Mr. Pherson delighted in sitting on the front porch of his home talking to passersby. He died in the house at age ninety-five. Many years later, when Diana Darnall and her husband took possession of the house, they found old mining tools and equipment in the cellar, a testament to Mr. Pherson's long mining career.

While psychic Krista Socash was interpreting the resident spirit in the home during the 1999 Historic Boulder Spirit Tour, some very interesting and bone-chilling events occurred that validated the home's history. According to Krista, a spirit immediately presented itself to her as a miner. Despite not knowing anything about the home before her visit, Krista sensed a hard-working man, very basic in his principles, who led a simple and honest life. Even though the spirit had never made itself known to Diana or her husband, it gave Krista very strong echoes of the past.

It was a delightful, crisp October evening as people began arriving at the house on Mapleton for the tour. As the first tour group entered the home, they assembled in the front room sitting in what was once the formal parlor. Krista stood by the front window as she described the essence of the man's spirit that inhabited the home. The window, which faces south, is framed by heavy velvet drapes. Directly to the left of the window hangs a beautiful pencil portrait of Mr. Pherson as a child. The portrait was found in the basement of the home by Diana, who later had it framed.

Krista's talk to the tour group was very basic and included the phrase "He led a very simple life" for in fact this was
the vibration she had sensed very strongly. The phrase, however, did not seem to please the spirit. As soon as she uttered
those words, the front porch light flickered and went out,
leaving the next group waiting on the porch in the dark.
Thinking the lightbulb had burned out, Krista continued her
talk as volunteers and those waiting in line scrambled to
replace the bulb.

When that group entered the front room they were treated to Krista's same interpretation of the spirit inhabiting the
house. Her talk didn't vary much and when she got to the
part about the man living a very simple life, the front porch
light flickered and went out once again. Krista silently made
the connection but the group had no idea what was happening.

When the next group of visitors entered and assembled in
the front room, Krista knew the spirit was disgruntled. This
time when she got to the "simple life" line, the brass tieback
holding the curtains fell out of the wall and came crashing to
the floor. The tour group jumped in fright and some, thinking it was just a bit too scary, left the room. Others stayed and
watched in fascination as Krista turned and spoke to the spirit directly, apologizing for misinterpreting his feelings. "I
realized that the spirit was not happy with the way I had
been describing him so I turned to where the tieback had fall-
en and spoke to him. I apologized for describing his life as
simple and all activity stopped. He made his point known."
The tieback that fell was located directly under the portrait of
Mr. Pherson.

The activity in the front room stopped, but there was

another presence in the house making itself known. A volunteer helping with tour groups was surprised by the strong scent of roses emanating from the back rooms of the home. Not a single rose was in sight yet Krista smelled the overpowering fragrance as well. "A female presence, not as prominent as the spirit in the front parlor, was near the library/TV room. She came and went throughout the night," Krista says.

Despite the crashing curtain tieback, Diana has always felt very positive vibrations about the house. It gives her a feeling of happiness and calm. But she also respects the fact that her house is still very much a part of the past, with a life of its own, and with spirits who still call the house on Mapleton their home. ❖

THE MYSTERY AT MACKY

Chapter 9

THE MYSTERY AT MACKY

Some say that late at night, passersby have heard blood-curdling screams coming from Macky, when the building is dark, and presumably no one is there.

Macky Auditorium on Boulder's University of Colorado campus is one of the most publicly recognized buildings in Boulder. Each year, thousands of students study various subjects in its classrooms, and a far larger number of local citizens attend concerts, plays, the opera, and special events in its first-rate auditorium. Given all that history and character, it's easy to forget that Macky is also home to the ghost of Elaura Jeanne Jaquette—the victim of one of Boulder's most notorious crimes.

Construction of Boulder's premiere concert hall began in 1909 after Andrew J. Macky, President of Boulder's First National Bank, died and left $300,000 to build an auditorium. Problems with Macky's estate stalled the construction, which took thirteen years to complete. When Macky Auditorium finally opened, audiences were significantly impressed with its size, the amber glass windows, and carved plaster ornamentation. Since then, the 2,000-seat auditorium has featured classical and popular musical concerts, dance performances, lectures, and films. Sweeping in and out of the auditorium through the massive front doors, concert-goers are directed to their seats on either the main floor or in the balcony. Few are aware that from the third floor on both sides of the building small doors open into a narrow spiral staircase that climbs to yet another floor. Certainly there was no reason to know that in 1966, because only select people were issued keys to the "towers."

The ivy-covered towers are small, L-shaped rooms, more a result of the unique architectural design rather than a specific utilitarian function. Still, when the music school near the campus Memorial Center became overcrowded and the organ department needed space, the towers were put to use. The main area on the second floor of the east wing accommodated offices, classrooms, and two organs, while the basement housed two more organs, and nicely enough, there was more than adequate space for an organ in each of the towers. Approximately fifty music students were issued keys to the tower and another fifty went to teachers, administrators, and a custodian or two.

It was quiet in the towers. An organ student could spend many happy hours there practicing without interruption. It was also perfect rehearsal space because others in the building weren't disturbed. The towers were nearly sound proof. It was that out-of-the-way location that proved fatal for twenty-year-old Elaura Jaquette, murdered in Macky's west tower on a hot summer afternoon in 1966.

"The murder changed the psychology of the campus," says longtime CU employee Alan Cass. "It was a frightening experience for everyone because until then it was a safe place."

Since the murder, stories of Elaura Jaquette's return to the campus have proliferated, generating Boulder's own "phantom of the opera" tale. Some say that late at night, passersby have heard blood-curdling screams coming from Macky, when the building is dark, and presumably no one is there. Others have heard the distant echo of organ music coming from the tower, even though the organ is locked and the room is now office space.

Jaquette had come to Boulder from Grand Junction to major in zoology. She had just completed her junior year, and rather than return to the Western Slope for the summer, she agreed to live with a Boulder family and baby-sit their four children. Described by friends as quiet and sweet, Jaquette was a member of the Campus Crusade for Christ, sang in church choirs, and played the piano. "She was happy when she got up in the morning and happy when she went to bed," her aunt, Violet Borge, told reporters.

On the afternoon of July 9, Jaquette had taken the children to the Flatirons Theater near campus, in an area known as University Hill. The boys later told police that Elaura had planned to do a little bird watching and sketch squirrels at a grassy area near Macky. When the movie ended, the children were surprised when Jaquette wasn't there to meet them. They knew, however, that she was headed to the campus, so they walked to an area near Varsity Pond where they had picnicked in the past. They didn't find Jaquette, just her white sneakers, a pair of binoculars, a binocular case, an orange, potato chips, a sandwich, and the wristwatch of one of the four boys she was babysitting.

Late that afternoon, another CU student entered Macky's west tower and found Jaquette's battered and beaten body. Police reports described the walls as being smeared with blood. A single, bloody palm print on a wooden plank found lying across Jaquette's body eventually helped an FBI special agent identify the killer. After four long weeks, police traced the crime to a thirty-seven-year-old custodian named Joseph Dyer Morse, a Longmont father of five. Morse pleaded not guilty. There was just one palm print, but at the trial one of Morse's daughters testified that her father returned home with bloody clothes the day of the murder and asked her to wash them.

Morse was sentenced to life in prison but maintained his innocence until 1980, when he admitted to the parole board that he had killed Jaquette. In 1966, prisoners convicted for life were allowed to apply for parole ten years after the crime. To prevent that from happening, Boulder prosecutors have remained diligent, annually urging the parole board to keep Morse, now more than seventy years old, behind bars until the day he dies.

One thing that's still puzzling is how Morse got Jaquette to leave her personal belongings behind, and follow him to the tower. The two were not strangers—Morse knew Jaquette from her summer job at CU's admissions office. There's speculation that he saw her sitting on the grass, wandered over and struck up a conversation. She was from a small town where violent crime was rare, so it's easy to believe she may have been lured to the tower because of her trusting nature. But what did he tell her? What could have been so urgent that Jaquette was willing to abandon her binoculars, shoes, and other personal items?

It's the piece of the story that still fascinates Cass, the Macky stage manager at the time of the murder. "She was a zoology major, so perhaps he said he'd found an injured animal. She was very responsible, so it must have been a pretty good story to lure her up there."

Unwittingly, Cass became the unofficial historian of the Jaquette case. He has repeatedly asked Morse for an interview to learn the full story, but has always been turned down. "Macky had always been a wonderful concert hall, and so we took the murder rather personally."

After the murder, the room was cleaned up and organ majors continued to practice in the west tower, or at least some of them did. "It was creepy," says a student from the mid-70s. "Often it was the only practice room available but I'd go home and play the piano rather than go up there. I never saw a ghost, but the tower felt like it was far, far away from the rest of building. It didn't feel like that in the east tower. The west tower had a sort of timeless feeling—like it wasn't connected to the rest of the campus. It was easy to forget that on the floor below, students were coming and going from classes. I didn't know any of the details of the murder—the instructors didn't like to talk about it, but it wasn't a pleasant place. Even when I was playing church hymns, something that should have been comforting, I was always looking over my shoulder."

Other organ students swore they could still see blood on the walls—that the walls hadn't been properly painted or that the paint mysteriously washed off. Still others said that the blood-stained keys of the organ remained impossible to clean. A distinct dent on the organ's lower right side was never repaired and detectives said it was caused when Morse swung the wooden plank at Jaquette.

Eerie claims about the building have continued for nearly four decades. It's impossible to say how long it's been there, but on the wall next to the entrance of the west tower where Jaquette was killed someone has written these words:

R.I.P.
Elaura Jaquette
May this room remain peaceful
Amen

❖

The dead fed you
Amid the slant stones of graveyards.
Pale ghosts who planted you
Came in the night-time
And let their thin hair blow through your clustered stems.

———————————

"Lilacs"
Amy Lowell

Clinton Otis Dumm

THE OBSESSIVE BOY SCOUT

Chapter 10

THE OBSESSIVE BOY SCOUT

Some who normally worked late hours began leaving early, sensing that someone or something was in the building after hours.

It started with the display lights at Boulder's old Pioneer Museum. They began turning on and off by themselves. Employees said something felt bad—as though there was suddenly a presence at the museum that was not there before. Some who normally worked late hours began leaving early, sensing that someone or something was in the building after hours. And then there were the phones. Callers reported that they'd spoken to a very nice gentleman on the phone after the museum had closed for the day. But there wasn't any gentleman answering phones at the museum. Unless it was Clinton Dumm.

Clinton Otis Dumm came into the world on February 17, 1892. He was the first child born to James Dumm and Sue Caton in a house located on the north side of Flagstaff Mountain. A homesteader who arrived in Colorado by covered wagon, James Dumm bought an orchard on Flagstaff, as well as a 150-acre farm near Longmont. A second son died at eight months and a third son, Wylie, was born in 1898.

Only six years separated them in age, but the Dumm brothers couldn't have been less alike. Clinton was fair with sparse and wispy hair. He was soft spoken and had an effeminate air some found uncomfortable. Not the pioneering type his father had likely expected.

Wylie, on the other hand, was all that his father could have hoped for. Handsome and rugged, he was a basketball star and champion swimmer at the State Preparatory School (now Boulder High). When World War I broke out, he joined the Navy and served on the U.S.S. Leviathon. He looked spectacular in a uniform.

All that would have been unsettling for Clinton, who for unexplained reasons was unable to join the Navy. He remained in Boulder working as a photo finisher in the darkroom of Yocum Studios. Without a Navy uniform or a job that would allow him to wear one, Clinton became obsessed. He wanted to belong to something. He wanted to wear a uniform, and he found an interesting way to do so. He joined the Boy Scouts.

A grown man joining the Boy Scouts seems unlikely today, but scouting was new at that time and open to adults as well as children. Both adults and children worked their way up the ranks—a very appealing aspect to Clinton since it reminded him of the military.

Clinton had found his place in the world, and was enormously successful as a scout. He was soon the scoutmaster of Boulder's Troop 71 and worked diligently toward the goal of attaining every merit badge possible. He collected more than seventy badges, including Eagle Scout in 1928.

But as you might guess, not everyone was comfortable with a forty-six-year-old man obsessed by scouting and still living at home with his mother. People were suspicious and intolerant and in 1938, Clinton was forced out of the Scouts. If that wasn't heartbreak enough, it was followed by his mother's death later that year. Clinton often told acquaintances, "I lost my mother and my troop in the same year." He called losing his troop "the major disappointment of my life."

That disappointment made Clinton a recluse and eccentric. He talked only of scouting, and was sometimes seen on the periphery of scouting events wearing his merit badge sash over his suit. While the newspaper ran stories about the success of his brother Wylie—he later became a banker in California—they ran jokes about Clinton. Armed with scrapbooks full of old comic strips, he roamed the streets wearing his scouting uniform, living in the past.

Clinton Dumm died at the age of seventy-eight on September 19, 1970. His funeral service included a Boy Scout color guard.

The Boy Scouts had unceremoniously forgotten Clinton during his life, but they took more interest in him after his death. Overlooking his strange reputation, they went to his house in search of scouting history and memorabilia they knew he had collected over the years.

Bob Bradfield was then the Arapahoe District Scout commissioner and remembers that like the man himself, Dumm's house was incomprehensible, a maze of passages. An ancient racing car occupied most of the basement, a car that Clinton had built. It still ran. There were sophisticated model airplanes and stacks of old newspapers. Inside crates that lined the walls of the house, Clinton stored his detailed mechanical renderings. One of Dumm's renderings, a pen and ink blueprint of the locomotive in Boulder's Central Park, was so accurate it could have been used to construct the machine. The simple-minded man appeared to be something of a mechanical genius.

Mixed in with the rest of it, the scouts found Clinton's uniform along with a wide-brimmed hat, a delicately embroidered merit sash, ancient membership cards, and other relics. Unsure what to do with the keepsakes, Bradfield took them to his home for storage.

Shortly thereafter, unexplained events began happening at the Bradfield's home. "At first, it was nothing you could put your finger on," Bradfield told *Boulder Magazine*. Little things, like pilot lights going off when there had never been a problem before. The incidents became so numerous that the Public Service Company was called but couldn't trace the cause.

One day when Bradfield's wife was home alone, a sudden violent crash rocked the house. It was centered in her son's room. A stereo that had been set securely on a shelf was lying in the center of the room, as if someone had swept an arm across the shelf in a violent outburst. Only one object remained undisturbed: Clinton Dumm's merit sash.

Bradfield decided the Dumm artifacts would be better off at the Boulder Historical Society. The chaotic events at his house stopped and just as quickly began at the Society's museum. Flickering lights, an unnerving presence, and reports of a "nice gentleman" answering the phones after hours were commonplace.

The museum was nonetheless thrilled to have a scouting uniform in such pristine shape and used a mannequin to display the old man's prized possession. It occupied a prominent place at the museum, especially during National Boy Scout Month. But when curators moved the mannequin to make room for another exhibit honoring the Girl Scouts, things got a little strange.

Leanne Sander was the museum's director from 1979 to 1983 and tells the following story. "I remember looking back at the mannequin as I was locking up that night and thinking, 'Old Clint isn't going to be too happy about this,'" Sander told the *Boulder Magazine*. "The next morning I found the Girl Scout display in a shambles on the floor. Some of it had been destroyed and some had been thrown to the center of the room. It was like someone had thrown a fit but a fit with specific intent." Sander said nothing else at the museum had been touched.

Clinton Otis Dumm had finally seen his scouting contributions honored. And he would not be denied. ❖

PHANTOMS IN LEFT HAND CANYON

Chapter 11

PHANTOMS IN LEFT HAND CANYON

Nocturnal visitors hover over beds or pause in bedroom doorways. Other spirits turn on lights, open doors, stomp through bedrooms, or sit down at the typewriter.

I n a more than 100-year-old stone house in Boulder's Left Hand Canyon, Tom Hoh and other family members have gotten used to their frequent visitors from another realm. But Tom never meant to believe in ghosts. "I was always very logically oriented toward mathematics and engineering." That was more than thirty years ago. Before the Ouija board incident.

An engineering consultant, Hoh set out with his former wife Laurie to prove that communicating with spirits through a Ouija board was nonsense. Such "talking boards" had been around since the 19th century, but a slick version of the game produced by Parker Brothers in 1966 had caught the attention of a new generation. Tom was eager to proclaim it was nothing more than hocus-pocus.

Sitting in front of a recently repaired fireplace, Tom and

Laurie were shaken, however, when the board unexpectedly spelled out a message—"The fire feels fantastic. It's nice to have that fireplace working again." The message was signed with the initials, R.G.S., the same initials that appear on a slab of concrete in the basement—the initials of the home's deceased former owner. After that, the spirits that frequent Hoh's house needed little encouragement.

Soon Hoh began to awaken in the night to the sight of "fairly classic" ghostly figures hovering over his bed. According to Hoh, "As my fear would build, they would migrate through the wall." The figures, usually men, were sometimes strangers or deceased friends and relatives. Hoh says they nearly always entered from the north wall and migrated out the west wall.

"These things almost always happen when I'm alone in the house, and nearly always between the hours of three and four a.m.," says Hoh. "One night a woman came toward the foot of my bed from the adjoining bathroom. She stopped and looked at me, and then put her hand in mine. I was surprised because her hand was warm. Again, because I woke up from a deep sleep I wasn't afraid at first. But as she held my hand I became fearful and she disappeared."

After living in the house for thirty-five years, Hoh doesn't get overly excited about any of this. In fact, he has subsequently embraced the belief that what happens in the universe doesn't always have a logical explanation. He has studied these beliefs with researcher and inventor Robert A. Monroe, founder of the Monroe Institute and a proponent of out-of-body explorations. Monroe has documented hundreds of paranormal incidents similar to the ones described by Hoh. "I think it's as much me as the house. I suspect I found the house or it found me because I had my antenna up for being open to these kind of experiences."

Whatever it is, nocturnal visitors hover over beds or pause in bedroom doorways. Others spirits turn on lights, open doors, stomp through bedrooms, or sit down at Hoh's typewriter. Over the years, the spirits have used a number of ways to get attention. Laurie would hear footsteps in the empty house every time she went into the cellar. One night water valves were inexplicably reversed.

Still, the family has made no attempt to exorcise the house and Tom does not intend to. "Nothing bad has ever come of any of this stuff. I am convinced there is a whole network of external creatures that do exist and visit us from time to time," says Hoh. "I don't know if I'd call them ghosts; I don't like that term. I think they pass on clues, warnings, red flags, ideas, flashes of inspiration. They will do anything to pass on information to other seekers."

In fact, Tom credits messages from another plane with saving his life more than once. One evening Hoh was awakened three times by the vision of a helmet with an oval emblem on the front. "I kept dreaming the same dream over and over but I couldn't get close enough to read what the helmet's emblem said." The next day as he rode his motorcycle into town, Hoh spotted a helmet with the exact emblem lying beside the road. "When I stopped to investigate, I found a note inside the helmet that read, 'life is fragile—handle with care.'"

In those days, Hoh liked to drive fast. He was racing his motorcycle home the following evening when he reached the spot where he had found the helmet, remembered the note, and abruptly slowed down. "I came around the corner and there was the largest herd of deer I had ever seen, or have yet to see again in the canyon. I was still going too fast, weaving in and out of the herd, but I had slowed down enough to avoid a major crash."

Motorcycles and waterbeds seemed to go hand-in-hand in the mid-70s and Tom had one of each. One morning at exactly 3:52 a.m., Tom sat up in bed terrified. He had been dreaming that his waterbed was leaking and he was about to be electrocuted. He got out of the bed and saw that a slow trickle of water was making its way toward an electrical outlet in the floor. Although water is not typically a good conductor of electricity, the ionized water in the waterbed would have been. "The only thing that prevented the water from getting to that outlet faster than it did was the fact that the wooden floors had been waxed that day, and the water had beaded-up along the floorboards. If I hadn't been awakened, I would have been dead within minutes."

On a third occasion, Hoh was roused from a vivid dream about a fire and the feeling that something was hovering over him. "I sensed that something was wrong in the basement, but I didn't get up. There were no lights on in the house and I don't know, I just didn't get up." In the basement the following morning, Tom discovered that a short piece of old aluminum wiring had caused the electrical box to overheat and it had started a small fire. The fire had climbed the fireplace wall and then died out on its own. "Again, something was trying to warn me. I think the entities talk louder to me."

Hoh had pretty much accepted the paranormal activity in his house when on one occasion he became the object of a ghostly tug-of-war. "There were two people on either side of me and they were arguing about me. One was saying, 'He's ready,' and the other was saying, 'No, he's not.' I remember looking from one to the other and again, the moment I became fearful, they were gone." Tom believes the spirits were arguing over whether he was ready to experience another plane of consciousness.

"I think I'm just a conduit, a channel, a door for a network of other dwellers. You have to be curious, receptive to perceiving them. I like to think of life as an exam, and fortunately I haven't had to hand in my test yet. My beliefs are still forming. To me it's arrogant and dangerous to think we know everything about the universe, or that everything can be explained. We aren't receptive to learning if we think we know the answers."

Hoh also wonders if the area where his house is located could be a focal point for psychic occurrences because it was once home to the Arapaho Indians, including Chief Left Hand (his Arapaho name was Niwot). Some say Chief Niwot cursed the Boulder Valley when he reportedly said: "It is so beautiful that people seeing it will want to stay and their staying will be the undoing of the beauty." Hoh believes Chief Niwot's words have been misinterpreted. "I think it was a warning, not a curse. It was more like, once you have spent time here, and you leave, something will always be missing and you'll feel a need to return."

Apparently someone knows the welcome mat is always out at Tom Hoh's house. ❖

THE HAUNTINGS ON PINE STREET

Chapter 12

THE HAUNTINGS ON PINE STREET

"Ghost, daddy," the boy said. They both shivered because of the sudden cold and looked up to see the filmy image of a woman standing before them.

In July of 1996, when the Middletons moved into their home on Pine Street with their young family in tow, they had no idea that they would be sharing the house with its resident spirits. As they went about settling into their two-story, foursquare-style home, there were no obvious signs that there were spirits about. But Kathryn Middleton immediately had a feeling, a sense that there was more to the house than they realized.

It was about two-to-three months later when the flickering of the master bedroom light fixture began at about the same time every night. Kathryn remembers the approximate time the flickers started and how she would try to tie them in with the heater coming on, or the dishwasher, or any other thing that might make the energy fluctuate. It was an old house after all. Though the pattern continued at the same time every night, it did not coincide with the refrigerator or other appliances activating. The flickers persisted.

The home was built in 1904, and the Middletons are the ninth owners. Kathryn had a clear idea of who her resident ghost was when the hauntings started. "I just had a feeling it was the woman who lived in the home from the late '40s through 1989. When we moved in, I also heard from neighbors that a woman had convalesced in what is now the dining room but I didn't have any more details."

The hauntings began to increase and Kathryn began to feel some activity on the stairs. "I always felt as though there was someone on the stairs behind me, and when I'd go down to get the baby a bottle I'd even run back up the stairs because it felt kind of creepy." Then one day she saw the image of a woman in a red robe on the landing of the stairway and her suspicions were confirmed.

The energy on the stairs was also validated by her husband James, who up until that point had been somewhat skeptical. One night, while carrying his then two-year-old son up the stairs, they encountered an area of freezing cold air on the first landing. "Ghost, daddy," the boy said. They both shivered because of the sudden cold and looked up to see the filmy image of a woman standing before them. The woman appeared to be older and was dressed in white. James particularly remembers her high-collared white blouse. The image then disappeared. He was now a believer in the ghost his wife had been describing. The little boy, on the other hand, seems to have accepted the spirit's presence in the home from the very beginning.

During the summer of 2000, the Middletons were knee-deep in a major remodeling of the home and actually moved out so the construction could be completed. Wallpaper was removed, walls were moved, and bathrooms were redone. The remodel was quite extensive.

One morning, Kathryn came by the home with her two sons and stood outside on the front sidewalk, watching them play before she entered to talk with the workmen. "I felt the strangest sensation that someone was watching me from my front window," she says. Slowly she turned and faced the house. In the bottom right corner of the front picture window was the face of a woman. "She was wearing a white, high-collared blouse and her hair was pulled back severely. Obviously I was startled and I got the immediate impression that she was angry at me for remodeling the house. That was what she looked like."

Thinking someone might have entered the home during the construction, Kathryn gathered the children and went upstairs to one of the bedrooms where a workman was working behind a door. "Seen any ghosts today?" she asked him jokingly. The man put down his tools and looked up at her in disbelief. "Funny you should say that," he said. "I've had the strangest sensation that someone has been in this room deliberately closing this door all morning. Every time I opened it, it closed. I was getting ready to take it off its hinges and rehang it."

With the construction completed, the family moved back into the home and the ghost activity resumed. On one particularly late night, after spending a long day preparing for her son's birthday, Kathryn was walking down the hallway with a lightbulb in her hand when a force sent it shattering against the wall. "I could feel the force as though someone had deliberately knocked it right out of my hand," she says. "That has been the only incident of the ghost being mean." By this time Kathryn was familiar with the ghost but this incident startled her because it was out of character. Tired, she cleaned up the mess and went to bed.

The other indication of resident spirits is evident in the living room where an obnoxious odor, a cross between sulfur and dead fish, can be smelled in the corner from time to time. The Middletons assumed it was in the old carpeting but cleaning did nothing to remove the odor which comes and goes. Kathryn says that during the remodel the carpet was torn out of the room, all but assuring that the smell would vanish. She was wrong. While the odor hasn't been noticed for some time, it lingered even after the remodeling.

Psychic Krista Socash did an interpretation of the spirits in the home and was able to verify a lot of what the Middletons had been experiencing. However, in addition to a woman on the stairs, Krista felt the strong presence of a young girl near the small bedroom at the top of the stairs. "It seems like the woman on the stairs is waiting for someone, perhaps a suitor," Krista says. "She seems to be thinking about a decision she has made about marriage. She left the home at an early age and has come back after her death."

The spirit of the young girl near the little bedroom, which was a closet before the remodeling, is of particular interest to Kathryn because that is the room of her eighteen-month-old daughter. Krista sensed that the young spirit loved little children and that she had a very playful presence. "I have often felt that the energy in my daughter's room was so different from that in the rest of the house," Kathryn says. "It has always seemed so feminine and very nurturing." Initially her son slept in the room but he never slept well. So Kathryn moved him to the other bedroom and made the little room a nursery for her daughter. It seems to have been the right choice. On several occasions she has been surprised when her daughter seems to be playing with someone in her crib and doesn't want to be taken out. As Kathryn left her daughter's room at bedtime recently, she suddenly felt a rush of extremely cold air at her feet. "I knew it was the spirit going into my daughter's room. I just said 'OK, leave her alone now, it's her bedtime,' and the air vanished."

Whereas Kathryn and her family had only sensed ghost activity in the lower level of the home, on the stairs, and sometimes in her daughter's room, Krista, in her psychic assessment, found spirit energies of differing natures throughout the house. During her visit, Krista felt the presence of a bitter, angry, older woman downstairs in the dining room area. Was she the one peering from the window during the remodel? Krista suggests that while spirits are not typically angry about remodels they do feel "lost" because of the changes made to the home.

Krista also felt the spirit of an older man in the living room, in the northeast corner to be exact. A framed picture hangs above where he sits and according to Kathryn, the picture is crooked every day, even after repeated efforts to straighten it. "He's playing with you," Krista told Kathryn. "He's making himself known." This particular spirit gave Krista a sense of being disapproving and upset. "He is someone's father and he's disapproving of his family's lifestyle. He is also irritated by a female presence in the house. Krista tied the odor in the living room directly to the male spirit.

The hallway that runs from the front entrance of the home

to the bright, cheerful kitchen was another hot spot for Krista. "The energy there is very heavy and dark," she says. One almost feels the urge to run through it to get into the kitchen. Interestingly, Kathryn's husband constructed a small office nook off the hallway, but grew to experience discomfort and uneasiness if he spent any amount of time there. According to Krista this is very understandable. She sensed a fight had occurred outside of the office and that the spirit of a sick little boy was present. Her advice? Move the office to the cellar.

The cellar, on the other hand, has a fun, almost jovial atmosphere, very different from the rest of the house. It has become a storage room of sorts, as most cellars are, and James feels at home there. Whenever the Middletons have a party all the men seem to congregate in the cellar, also not surprising to Krista. She immediately sensed a male spirit in the cellar, a spirit who enjoys fun and games. Kathryn tried to put her sewing room in the cellar but it just didn't feel right. The cellar now belongs to the men.

Research on the house shows that it was built by James Park and his wife, Mary B. Park. Mr. Park was a local banker who retired in 1910. An historic building inventory report states that Mr. Park died in California in 1947. The house subsequently had eight more owners until the Middletons moved in. During the writing of this book, Kathryn spoke with a ninety-year-old neighbor, a retired physician who vividly remembered making house calls to the Pine Street home in the 1950s. According to the physician, one woman resident of the home was very sullen and seemed unhappy, perhaps due to the fact that she was asthmatic and was housebound for many years.

Even with their resident spirits the Middletons enjoy their home. "This is the type of house I have always dreamed of," Kathryn says. "I will live here forever. I enjoy the spirits in my home." The old house on Pine is obviously in good hands. And Kathryn has a sympathetic spirit. It is a situation that could lead to the discovery of many more secrets and perhaps many more ghosts. ❖

Author's note: I worked on setting up meetings with Kathryn and Krista for approximately a two-week period. During that time I was also doing historical research on the home. The research was hard to come by and initially I was stuck with basic information which included the fact that the home was built in 1904. I had a sheet of paper with the information about the house next to my computer. After we met at the home, I was surprised to get a call from a friend who wondered why in the world my e-mails were coming to her with such strange dates. I immediately went to my "send" file and found that all of the e-mails I had been sending out during that time had gone out with the wrong date. My teenage son came to my aid and went to the desktop setup to determine the source of the problem. Sure enough, the date on the computer was no longer 2002 but somehow had been set to 1904. – A.A.L.

Ready to Travel the Narrows

SHORT BUT SPOOKY

Chapter 13

SHORT BUT SPOOKY

The Narrows

Traveling west up Boulder Canyon, motorists on Highway 119 find a popular tourist attraction—Boulder Falls. While certainly modest in comparison to many, Boulder Falls nonetheless creates a magnificent spectacle as water crashes over huge rocks. And amazing sounds. Some say, otherworldly sounds.

Construction of a road through Boulder Canyon by way of the Narrows was started in 1869 after silver was discovered at Caribou—now a ghost town some twenty-two miles west of Boulder.

Before the road, traveling from the mines to Boulder could be dangerous. In those days, miners transported ore to town in heavy wagons pulled by teams of plodding horses. The trail was steep at the Narrows, so steep that teamsters tied logs to the wagons to keep them from overrunning the horses. And here lies the setting for reports of a rather frightful haunting.

One icy winter night, an unfortunate Irish teamster had tied logs to the wagon anticipating the treacherous descent. But the logs hit a patch of ice and began skidding toward the wagon. The driver, in a desperate attempt to save his cargo and his life, whipped up the team to a mad gallop trying to outrun the rushing logs. But the team of horses, sweating and foaming at the mouth, failed to negotiate the slippery terrain. The race ended with the driver and his team dead, the wagon shattered against the canyon wall.

That should be the end of the story, except for witnesses who say those last few moments are occasionally replayed in the winding canyon. At a certain bend in the road near Boulder Falls, snatches of a raucous Irish ballad have been heard along with the sound of jolting wheels, the screams of frightened horses, and a final crash. ❖

The Woman in White

What is the mystery behind the woman in the long white dress? For years, residents of Chautauqua have reported seeing such a figure wandering through the park, her broad-brimmed hat shading her eyes from the sun. One of Boulder's oldest ghost stories, the legend of the woman in white is still popular today.

Boulder's Chautauqua was built in 1898 as a summer retreat for Texas schoolteachers, eager to escape their state's heat and dust. They found the Boulder climate more agreeable and in 1897, a group of Texas professors encouraged city leaders to propose the chautauqua to Boulder's citizens. City council, in turn, asked residents to approve bond money to buy land, provide water, and electricity. Boulder voters embraced the chautauqua concept, and approved the bonds overwhelmingly.

Soon construction was underway on a beautiful parcel of land at the base of the Flatirons. Forty-five days later, the Chautauqua Auditorium and Dining Hall stood facing a meadow where the Texans would pitch tents for several years before building small seasonal cabins around the perimeter of what is known as Chautauqua Park. It was the turn of the century and Americans were hungry for new ideas and forms of entertainment. They wanted to hear lectures, politicians, and musicians. With the Chautauqua built, Democratic leader and orator William Jennings Bryant, evangelist Billy Sunday, social reformer Jane Addams, and the John Phillip Sousa Band, among others, made their way to Boulder. The original Chautauqua in New York State and the Boulder Chautauqua were once two of 8,000 thriving in the United States. Now just a few remain.

The early chautauquas ascribed to this motto: "...a place in which to grow spiritually, a place of intellectual stimulation, where faith is restored and the arts are valued..." In her book, *A Look at Boulder*, Phyllis Smith says the word chautauqua is actually an Indian word meaning "foggy place" while others say it means "place where a child was washed away." Some people still recognize the Algonquin Indian meaning, "bag tied in the middle," which is the shape of Lake Chautauqua in New York.

Another derivation of the word chautauqua, according to Smith, is "a place of easy death," a possible explanation for why the woman in white always looks so content. Professional ghost hunters say that spirits don't always return to haunt *tragic* sites, but instead return to recall the good old days.

So why wouldn't she want to stay? She silently strolls the quaint streets of Boulder's Chautauqua, parasol and gloves in hand, not bothering anyone but also not giving any hint of why she continues to haunt the beautiful park. ❖

Divine Intervention

An unsolved murder, a famous movie star, a beautiful girl, and drugs...all the trappings for a Hollywood movie, and for a Boulder ghost story few have heard anything about.

In the late 1990s, Hope Hewetson, a psychic from Boulder's Psychic Horizons, received a phone call from three young men living in Spanish Towers. They wanted an explanation for the strange things happening in their apartment. The Towers is a complex near the CU campus typically occupied by university students.

Hewetson didn't live in Boulder in 1983 and therefore didn't know that in August of that year, a promising CU student named Sid Wells was murdered in his apartment at the Towers, killed by a single shotgun blast to the back of his head.

"The young men said they experienced unexplained noises, flickering lights, and other phenomena that made them nervous," Hewetson says. The psychic came to feel that the spirit causing these disturbances was that of a young man who had died a violent death in the apartment. Only later did she learn the story of Sid Wells.

"The spirit was there to warn the boys, aware that they were doing stupid things that could ruin their lives. It was more divine intervention than a haunting," says Hewetson.

From the first moments of the police investigation it was obvious this would be one of Boulder's rare murders. But in the wee hours of the morning, police were unaware that reporters would soon descend on Boulder and the murder would draw international publicity.

Soon word was out that the twenty-two-year-old Wells was a journalism student at CU, and more importantly to reporters, he was the boyfriend of CU student Shauna Redford, the daughter of actor Robert Redford. Redford was filming "The Natural" when the murder occurred and shut down the set to attend Wells' funeral in Longmont. Curious reporters and photographers nearly outnumbered those present for the service.

By that time an investigation was well underway although from the start the murder seemed cut-and-dried. Thayne Alan Smika, who shared the apartment with Wells, was the prime suspect. There were no signs of forced entry to the condominium and no indication that a struggle took place. A search of Smika's home in Akron, Colorado, turned up a 20 gauge shotgun and pellets believed to be a possible match to those that killed Wells. Also, Smika's mother told police her son may have had some involvement in the murder and that he suffered from blackouts or seizures, and could not always control or remember his actions.

As to a motive, police initially thought it was drugs, after a small trace of cocaine was found during the coroner's autopsy. Eventually that theory was abandoned and police now believe Smika killed Wells during an argument over unpaid rent.

No charges were filed against Smika at the time, however, because the Boulder County district attorney's office did not believe there was enough evidence to prosecute. Smika is believed to have changed his identity after fleeing an arrest for embezzlement in 1986 and his whereabouts are unknown.

"Ghosts are people who, for some reason, have elected to stay in this world," says Hewetson. "Their auras remain, because they were angry or upset when their physical bodies died.

"The spirit in the apartment was worried about where he saw the boys going with their lives. He believed they were involved in drugs and was fearful for them. The spirit was saying, 'You're doing some stupid things. Don't ruin your lives and end up like I did.' He wanted to make sure that his life had not been wasted—that someone could learn from his mistakes. He was interested in reincarnating but was trying to do something good before he left.

"After the spirit heard me relate this information to the three boys in the apartment, he was ready to go. He was ready to heal. He had accepted that it was necessary for him to have the kind of death he did in his lifetime but he also knew that he could choose differently next time. He just wanted to make sure that his message was heard, and it was." ❖

Grandpa in the Tuff Shed

E yebrows were raised when the story broke that baseball great Ted Williams was being cryogenically frozen upon his death in 2002—everywhere but in the town of Nederland, Colorado. The folks there know all about frozen bodies—more than they want to know. Until 1994, however, residents of the little mountain community sixteen miles west of Boulder had no idea that Bredo Morstoel was awaiting "reanimation" in a Tuff Shed just above town.

It was in the spring of that year that Morstoel's grandson, Trygve Bauge, was deported to Norway. His troubles with the law made local news headlines when *Daily Camera* reporter Clay Evans was sent to interview Bauge's mother. The elderly woman (Bredo's daughter) said she was worried as to how she would take care of the body—how she would afford the dry ice to keep Grandpa frozen. Evans gasped.

What was moments before a story about a deportation suddenly had a whole new angle.

Grandpa Bredo didn't die in Nederland, but rather at his family's chalet in Norway. Bauge had his grandfather's eighty-nine-year-old body transported to Los Angeles where it was cryogenically prepared, frozen, and eventually shipped to Colorado where Bauge was living. Bauge had started work on a concrete-covered, earthquake, fire and bombproof structure at the current site of the Tuff Shed, but finances were limited. He intended to have more than just Grandpa as a customer, and the main building would have connected to an underground vault where cryogenic capsules were to be stored. Bauge had in mind a round-the-clock monitored, high-tech facility. In the meantime, he was having dry ice delivered to keep the body frozen.

When the story broke to national attention, puzzled city officials were encouraged to act, to *do* something about the frozen Grandpa in the Tuff Shed. But what? Bauge hadn't committed a crime, so a local ordinance was revised prohibiting citizens from keeping a corpse on private property. But the law forbids making a current situation illegal, so Grandpa Bredo was "grandfathered" in, and the town ended its attempts to evict the body. Finally finding its sense of humor, the city of Nederland held a "Frozen Dead Guy Days" festival in 2002 and thousands turned out for coffin races, dead guy tours, a parade, and a look-a-like contest.

According to the Website www.deadfrozenguy.com, Grandpa has been a very popular guy with the media. His story has appeared in every local newspaper. He's been the subject of several television specials and reports have appeared in *The National Enquirer*. *National Geographic* featured Grandpa Bredo in an article and he was also the subject of an award-winning documentary.

Each month, Bo Shaffer, with a company called Delta Tech, delivers 800 pounds of ice to keep Grandpa "alive" in an aluminum box inside a styrofoam and plywood freezer where the temperature is around -60 degrees Fahrenheit. He regularly entertains curious reporters and psychics. In 1996, four Boulder psychics attempted to "read" Morstoel's wishes in the matter of remaining frozen. Each psychic entered the shed alone and compared notes afterward. "The biggest agreement we got was that Bredo didn't mind, but he thought it was a waste of money," Shaffer told the *Daily Camera*. "Why would he want that old decrepit body back?" The psychics concluded that Grandpa is mildly amused to slightly irritated.

In the meantime, the ice is delivered and Bauge pays the bill, vowing to eventually return to Nederland. He's still hopeful that future medical advances might someday bring Grandpa back to life—that he might be revived or cloned. More famous in death than life, the bizarre legacy of Grandpa Bredo lives on. ❖

Haunted Hotel

Guests enter the swinging doors of Boulder's grandest hotel to old-world elegance and timeless grace. The lobby and rooms at the Hotel Boulderado have been meticulously restored to their original Victorian elegance. The stained-glass canopy over the mezzanine delivers just the right amount of European sophistication and the intriguing classical-style stairwell is regularly the choice for young couples when it's time for the distinguished wedding photo. But there's more there than a colorful history and period furnishings. There are rumors of whispers in empty hallways, unexplained shadows, and mysterious visions.

Stories of ghosts at the Hotel Boulderado seem to have begun after a suicide there in 1924 and continue to live on.

"The third floor. If there's anything that feels odd in the hotel it's on the third floor," says Boulder historian Betty Chronic. "I've never had a sense of anything strange on the first floor or on the Mezzanine, but on the third floor I've had a feeling that there's a presence there, or several." Chronic says she's not fanciful enough to believe in ghosts or spirits but says she's too Irish to say there's no such thing.

"When the hotel was renting rooms as apartments to older residents during the 1960s, I used to visit an elderly woman who lived there. Her room was isolated, very separate from the rest of the hotel but she was happy living there, always content. It had a homey feeling, not at all scary. But there was a certain aura, a feeling in the hallways that caused me to think that spirits were looking on."

Even before the doors opened in 1909, sticks and stones were flying over what to name the hotel. William R. Rathvon was president of the Commercial Association at the time and many residents felt it should be named after him. Others liked Hotel Mack, in honor of A.J. Macky, president of the First National Bank. (The University of Colorado's auditorium was eventually named for Macky and has its own ghost.)

But Rathvon suggested a distinctly Colorado name—a combination of Boulder and Colorado, and came up with Boulderado.

In what is now typical Boulder fashion, a pen-and-ink firestorm ensued. The editor of the *Daily Camera*, L.C. Paddock, attacked the name viciously on the pages of the newspaper. "The word, Boulderado, is an offense against the English language and a rhetorical monstrosity."

But Rathvon argued for its individuality: "It will be the only hotel of that name in all the world, and if the name be copyrighted, it cannot be used for anything else without the consent of the hotel company. It stands for the city of Boulder in the state of Colorado. No matter when or where the words Hotel Boulderado may be heard by anyone who has ever rested beneath its roof, the city of Boulder, not Boulder in Montana, nor Boulder in Illinois, but Boulder in Colorado will instantly come to his mind whether it be one or twenty years after. And when he thinks of Boulder, he will remember the hotel. On the other hand, when the hotel comes to his mind, he will remember its name."

One couple apparently liked the sound of the name. On a warm evening in July of 1924, Lou Pfeiffer and his wife Mary Ellen took a train from Denver to Boulder and checked into the fifteen-year-old hotel. A pleasant enough looking pair, no one at the hotel knew that Lou Pfeiffer was out of work and suffering from chronic and likely fatal kidney trouble. With no reason to be suspicious, the clerk was unaware the middle-aged couple had registered under a fictitious name. Later, hotel staffers would learn that Lou and Mary Ellen had earlier made a suicide pact and chosen the Boulderado as their place to die.

But even as he signed the register, Lou was a step ahead of Mary Ellen. While she took a bath, her husband swallowed eight Veronal tablets, soaked some towels with chloroform, and lay down on the bed. When Mary Ellen came out of the bathroom she found her husband dead.

Mary Ellen's exit from the earthly plane proved far more difficult. Chloroform in hand, she followed her husband's example and lay down on the bed prepared to die. She apparently slipped into unconsciousness, but awoke hours later with a raging headache and burns on her face, neck, and back. Before heading out to the drug store for more chloroform, she carefully placed a note on the door that read, "Don't disturb, sick man in room."

Later, several employees said they saw her leave. A maid told police she had walked in a "wobbly manner" and noted something was wrong with her face. A bellboy reported that she had been "nervous and irritable."

Once at the druggist's, Mary Ellen asked for a pound of chloroform but was sold just four-ounces of the liquid anesthetic. She returned to the hotel and again tried to take her own life. Either the chloroform was too weak or Mary Ellen's will to live was too strong, because the second suicide attempt also failed. After another period of unconsciousness, she awoke, and made her way to a third store for more supplies. This time the pharmacist was wary and refused her order. She returned to the Boulderado, left her dead husband in the hotel room, and fled on the train back to Denver, leaving their luggage behind.

When hotel employees finally entered the Pfeiffer's room, they found Lou's body and contacted the coroner. The couple was soon identified from pictures, letters, and a library

100

card inside their luggage. Authorities eventually found Mary Ellen in a Denver hospital. In a bedside interview she said, "We were just two unlucky people who had grown tired of living. He (Lou) was all I had to live for. It was all a mistake I see clearly now. Instead of sympathizing with him in a desire to end it all, I should have diverted his mind."

The preliminary charges against Mary Ellen of aiding and abetting a suicide were dropped. Following a brief prayer service, Lou was buried in Boulder's Columbia Cemetery.

In the years that followed, guests such as Robert Frost, Helen Keller, and Louis Armstrong were among those who stayed at the hotel. The Boulderado's fortunes followed the nation's economy, and in the 1930s it went from being a luxury hotel to the cheapest place in town for those down on their luck and without a place to live.

Such was the state of the hotel in the summer of 1963, when a second suicide was reported. The manager made this statement to police:

"It was around the Fourth of July, and I thought I smelled gunpowder, but figured it was fireworks. Then a guest called me and asked me to look at something on the west fire escape. I found a man, fortyish, a carpenter from Pennsylvania, dead from a shotgun wound to the head. The receipt for the gun, purchased that day, was on the dresser. There was no note."

Four years later, an unfortunate third suicide occurred. The manager said, "A housekeeper was scared to death when she found a man, a young man worth a million with inherited money, who'd shot himself. Next to him was a big bottle of wine, a pipe of hash, and a .357 magnum revolver." Again, there was no note.

101

Finally in the late 1970s, renovation began on the landmark hotel and it was returned to its original splendor. The construction and remodeling has not, however, put an end to the ghosts or ghost stories. Guests continue to report sightings, even if they've never heard what others have said about the unnamed spirits.

In her book, *Legend of a Landmark, A History of the Hotel Boulderado*, Silvia Pettem recounts the following:

"On a recent visit to Boulder, a doctor and his wife checked into the hotel for the first time. The husband had a meeting to attend, so his wife entered the room alone at 10:30 a.m. She was given the same room that a few months earlier had been assigned to a spiritually oriented Native American. He had refused to stay in it because of a feeling he had when it was shown to him. But many other guests had come and gone in the interim with no comments.

"The doctor's wife, however, was happy with the room and felt comfortable upon arrival. She left and came back again and switched on a movie on television.

"'At noon I heard a woman's voice, and maybe a baby's in the room,' she said later. 'I wasn't scared, and the thought crossed my mind that some presence might be there, but I decided not to tell my husband or anyone else about it.'

"At 4:00 p.m. her husband arrived and switched the television to basketball. His wife explained that as a doctor, he was the last person in the world to believe in the supernatural, as he always had to have a scientific explanation for everything. No sooner had he heard a woman's voice, than he said to his wife, 'I think this place is haunted.' They both heard it again and could almost figure out what the voice was saying. They laughed about the incident and weren't

102

frightened.

"Then the doctor looked up and saw a 'white filmy thing' in the mirror of the dresser. Shaken up, he decided to have his first alcoholic drink of the day, and went into the other room of their suite to get some ice out of the refrigerator. As he opened the refrigerator door, a shadow crossed the coffee table in a place where no sun shone in. He tried for five minutes to create a similar shadow with his body before going back to the bedroom to tell his wife.

"She said later, 'My husband made a drawing of what he saw in the mirror, and although I didn't see it or the shadow, we both know they exist.' The couple spent the night in the same room with no further incidents.

"When they checked out the next morning, and told the sympathetic desk clerk what they had seen, they were amazed to find that other guests had reported similar experiences in the same, and only the same room."

Did one of the hotel's spirits pay a visit to the good doctor and his wife? Over the years, guests have reported doors opening and closing on their own, whispers and voices in seemingly empty hallways, and wispy apparitions seen, out of the corner of one's eye, disappearing through doorways and drapes. One guest reported feeling as though she was being followed, only to turn and find she was alone.

If there are ghosts in the Hotel Boulderado, they've never managed to frighten away the multitude of guests that come and go each year. These phantom spirits seem to enjoy the plush carpets and overstuffed furniture along with the rest of us as they continue to haunt Boulder's historic hotel. ❖

Shep's Grave Along the Turnpike   Photo by Tom Moen

Man's Best Friend

Since 1964, motorists traveling between Denver and Boulder have occasionally reported that a dog is stranded on the grassy hill next to the busy lanes of traffic near the Broomfield exit. No one has ever rescued the dog, however, and those who know the history of the Boulder-Denver turnpike will tell you that the apparition is likely Shep, a stray shepherd, long dead, that befriended the men who worked on the road more than fifty years ago.

It's almost unthinkable now, but there wasn't always a highway between Boulder and Denver. Talk began as early as 1912 about building a connecting road, but at the time the engineering problems seemed insurmountable. It wasn't until 1945 that serious discussion began about construction of a toll road. As historian Phyllis Smith writes in *A Look at Boulder*, "It was a project that would do more to change the face of Boulder than any local ordinance and, when finished, would be called the 'magic carpet to progress.'"

Colorado residents were cautious about the project because toll roads back East were in trouble and rarely paid for themselves. A consulting firm from Kansas was hired to conduct a feasibility study and, as expected, the report to the city council was discouraging. The firm concluded the road couldn't pay for itself until at least 1980, if at all. The Colorado General Assembly reviewed the report, rejected the dire predictions, and shortly thereafter authorized a bill to construct the highway.

By October 10, 1950, the first section of road had been graded. It was around that same time that a dog described as a shepherd-mix appeared one morning. The men expected the dog to return to its home at the end of the day, but when he was still there the next morning, the workers shared their lunch with their new friend. Before long, Shep was a fixture at the site and a beloved companion of the construction crew.

Two years later, in January of 1952, the Boulder-Denver Turnpike opened to traffic. Motorists paid ten cents to travel from Denver to Broomfield and twenty-five cents if their destination was Boulder. Daily customers or "commuters" knew the toll station operators by name and regularly called out a greeting to Shep, who shared the toll booth with them.

According to Smith, "When the toll station near Broomfield was finished, Shep took up residence there, carefully regarding each toll payer as he passed through. Shep was fed and cared for at the toll station for years and money was collected for Shep's occasional trips to the vet. The only time that Shep would not stay on duty was during the heavy traffic coming to Boulder for Saturday football games. On those occasions, Shep took up an observation post on a hillside, away from the cars."

Consultants were proven wrong about the Boulder-Denver Turnpike. The toll station closed on September 14, 1967, thirteen years ahead of schedule. Ironically, it was the country's first toll road to pay for itself.

Shep died in 1964, sparing toll station operators a decision about his future. He was buried just east of the Broomfield exit. His grave is marked by a stone of white marble, surrounded by a wrought-iron fence. It seems Shep kept his own playbook, and chose instead a phantom life haunting the road he had called home. Every day but game day. ❖

The Meditation Room

The hauntings at the house on Lincoln Place at first seemed so benign. Roommates Andy and Kate lived there in the late 1980s, and it didn't take long after they moved in for them to realize something was amiss. The three-bedroom home still stands in the neighborhood where elegant Tudor homes, small bungalows, and modern remodels coexist nicely.

They say the ghost activity began with air currents. Wind might be a better description for the mysterious drafts which blew through the house when no windows or doors were open. These drafts actually blew papers off tables, and with their sudden arrival Kate and Andy felt a presence had arrived. They could never explain it in words. Summer and winter, the drafts blew through the home. It was something they learned to live with, and even joked about.

The hauntings then began to take another form. The radio would start to play, not a result of anyone touching the actual radio, mind you, but in the wee hours, usually around two or three in the morning. The radio would come alive, at top volume, jolting Andy and Kate awake. Curiously, the radio stations in these middle-of-the-night hauntings were not the same stations listened to by the couple.

Then events took a turn for the worse. One evening, with houseguests in town, Kate offered her room to her visitors and went off to sleep in a small upstairs room. She called the room the "Meditation Room." It was square in size with a corner built out, probably for a vent or pipe of some sort. Kate still remembers the dream she was having that night when she was so rudely awakened. She was at a party, and she was happy and having a great time. She began to dream that her head was being lifted and at that point, her dream became reality. As she was sleeping, the ghost raised her body and threw her against the wall. Hitting the room's sharp corner, the blow of her body slamming against the wall awakened the guests in the next room who ran in to find her bleeding from the forehead.

Kate has never been able to explain the apparent sudden violence shown by the ghost, except that it was obviously upset that she was sleeping in the room. Needless to say, she never slept there again, and shortly afterwards Kate and Andy moved out of the house.

"After I was thrown, I entered that room more cautiously," Kate says. "We were scheduled to move a few weeks after it happened. I was definitely happy to be leaving."

To this day, the mystery of the Lincoln Place ghost and the meditation room on the upper floor remain just that, a mystery never to be solved. ❖

The Spirit on Spruce Street

"If the story dies, the ghost dies. They're like Tinker Bell—you have to keep clapping." So says Robert Lee Cook about his experiences at a house on west Spruce Street. Cook would appear to know what he's talking about. Now nearly eighty years old, he once collected more than a thousand stories in preparation for a book about ghosts. A writer and bookseller, Cook spent many hours on a bench in front of the Boulder County Courthouse listening to miners relate stories of the area's early mining days.

"My family lived in the house on Spruce Street for sixteen years through the 1950s and I was never able to find any substantial reason for the phenomena that went on in the corner of the living room. I investigated the history of the house to find a reason for a spirit to remain—something along the lines of revenge, retribution, jealousy, or unrequited love. I couldn't find anything so I figured it was just a family ghost," he says.

W. H. Nicholson, a former Houston oilman, built the Queen Anne-style home about 1891. The house has had several owners including Boulder's first mayor, F. C. Moys, a hardware dealer who owned the house from 1917 to 1920. After that, Robert L. Fink and his wife lived there for nearly twenty-five years and later, Homer Blacker, a farm implement dealer. Cook bought the house in 1948.

"We never heard anything about a ghost before we

moved in, but the folks who lived there previously were pretty traditional, old-line. I'd say I'm more of a romantic so maybe the spirit or spirits appeared because I didn't discount them. I can't say I believed or disbelieved. I just couldn't explain it."

The phenomena was concentrated in one corner that the Cook family found particularly cozy. When guests visited, however, they would sit in the corner for only a few minutes before complaining of a chill or feeling uncomfortable. The family's cat and dog avoided the area but would sit and stare into the corner for hours on end. Cook says that on several occasions the dog let out a shattering howl and dashed for the bedroom where he scrambled under the bed and refused to be calmed.

When Cook sold the Spruce Street home in the mid-1960s, the new owner told a similar story. "Usually nobody sits in that corner though there's a chair there. Nobody really gravitates toward the corner." Adding yet more mystery, a Boulder *Daily Camera* story quotes historian Jane Barker Valentine as saying: "Every year the residents receive a Christmas card addressed to 'Present Occupants.' The greeting says, 'We enjoyed living there.' The card is signed, 'From Former Occupants.'" Since Cook and the present occupants have been in possession of the house since the 1940s, the identity of these "former occupants"remains a mystery.

Cook maintains that Boulder's more intriguing ghost stories are dying off with the town's older storytellers. "Boulder is a very practical, very middle-class town without much sense of humor. Ghosts are only around as long as someone believes in them."

We believe. We believe. ❖

The House with Two Faces

Just a few doors from Boulder's famously haunted Castle House on University Hill, a two-story red brick home is a contrast in light and dark. Residents of years past used to descend the home's main stairway with a light foot, says psychic Krista Socash, glad to be alive, glancing out the front window with expectancy each morning. The positive energy in the front of the home contrasts sharply with that found in the back. Socash feels there were secrets there, perhaps illegal activity, people hurrying to get away, escaping from some sort of danger. The tenants feel it too.

Built in 1899, the grand house on Ninth Street is an example of Edwardian Vernacular architecture. There are large double-hung windows with transoms, stone sills and lintels, and gabled dormers. At some point in the 1970s, the house was remodeled into two dwellings and college students now occupy both halves.

This isn't a typical haunting, but a presence that sends chills through all who visit. "We moved to the front of the house last year because the back half gave us the creeps," says Heather, one of three roommates who rent the house. "I hated being there alone. It wasn't a good year. Since we've moved to the front of the house things have gone much more smoothly for all of us."

On the second floor there are two bedrooms, one of which Socash feels was a cheerful playroom when the house was first built. This is Courtney's room, but the three women all admit that they find themselves drawn there at all hours of the day just to hang around. It is unexplainable. In fact, Courtney is so content to spend time there that her roommates are forever trying to lure her out to join them on the first floor. "I believe that children spent a lot of happy hours there," says Socash. "It was a retreat from whatever was going on elsewhere on the property."

At the back of the house there's a large door in the ground that opens to steps leading to a basement, more like a cellar, that the women say continuously haunts them. "It's not so scary going down the stairs, it's just when you get down there you can't get out fast enough," says Allison. The feeling is ominous and unpleasant. A dark, unknown presence seems to lurk within the cellar walls.

Socash says this is the area where she senses that something was going on that wasn't on the up-and-up. Perhaps someone was selling moonshine, or illegal drugs at some point. "I can't tell you exactly what it was, but there's a very strong male presence and layers and layers of secrets."

The roommates tried to ignore the bad energy they say emanates from the basement and fix it up when they first moved in, but they gave up pretty quickly. "We had some people over for a party and some guys went down there and got into a wrestling match and trashed the place," says Heather. "They broke glasses and jars and other things. It seemed to be a bad omen. We had another roommate then who lived in the bedroom over the basement and she was an extremely unhappy person, and difficult to get along with. She felt she had to move out." Socash says the bad energy coming from the basement may have played a part.

"I sensed that the original family didn't have a lot of

money, but they had some for a while," says Socash. "So, they were constantly trying to get more money. Something was going on in the basement that was connected to their goal. I feel that something unpleasant happened there and that it is still affecting the energy at the back of the house."

From the street the house has a happy face, but venture around the corner to the back and the air is charged. There's a sadness there that no amount of time has been able to erase. And there are spirits who are still caught in their unpleasant plight. ❖

The Benevolent Ghost

I f there's such a thing as a benevolent ghost you will find her at Boulder's Mount St. Gertrude Academy. So well known was her spirit that the Academy became known as Boulder's most "famous" haunted building.

The Academy is now the city's premiere retirement community—a stately red brick structure at 970 Aurora Avenue on University Hill. Its recent reincarnation reveals little concerning the years when it was known for such mysteries as the sound of breaking windows, screams from the bell tower, and unexplained fires.

Four nuns from the Charity of Blessed Virgin Mary Abbey in Dubuque, Iowa opened the academy in 1892 as a school

The Academy Building

Carnegie Branch Library for Local History,
Boulder Historical Society Collection

for thirty students and a ward for nuns suffering from tuberculosis. According to its literature from that time, the school was founded on the principal of "fresh air and sunlight, wholesome and nutritious food, regular hours for rising and retiring and an abundance of healthful recreation and outdoor exercise" to promote the good health of the students. Sister Mary Theodore O'Connor led the group of nuns but regrettably became gravely ill and died at the school of tuberculosis, just one week before the building was finished. That as much as anything started ghost stories circulating even before the turn of the 20th century.

The nuns of her order kept Sister Mary's dream alive and the school operated for over three-quarters of a century. The dining room, kitchen, and pantries were on the ground floor. According to Therese Stengel Westermeier's book, *Mount Saint Gertrude: Ave Atque Vale*, the second floor housed female students and an infirmary for "Eastern pupils who are of delicate disposition," while the third floor was made up of parlors, music rooms, a study hall and a chapel. The fourth floor was devoted to dormitories and boarders.

"In those first days, the coyotes would come down from the canyon at night and howl about the place," Sister Mary Philomene said in her interviews with Westermeier. "This, together with a violent rattling of the windows, greatly frightened the sisters."

By 1969, Boulder had changed considerably and the girls school, profitable for so many years, crept into debt. At that time, the University of Colorado bought the property to house dance programs, its Bureau of Conferences and Real Estate and its Division of Continuing Education. But a mysterious fire in 1980 forced the university to close the building.

The roof on the fourth floor was destroyed along with other rooms inside the landmark. The fire ended any hopes the university had of turning it into offices. Empty and boarded-up, obscured by overgrown weeds and surrounded by chain-link fence, the Academy became an infamous spot for bon-fires, transients and vandals. Whole families of raccoons called the building home. Rumors of satanic activity and animal sacrifices were rampant. Neighbors reported sounds of screams from the bell tower and the shattering of glass in the middle of the night.

As early as 1981, the university began accepting development proposals. Debate over the Academy's future was heated, to put it mildly. Several proposals for redevelopment were promoted and swiftly rejected by either city officials or the surrounding neighborhood. Finally, in 1996, the plan for a retirement community was approved and renovation and new construction began.

The original wood and a mosaic floor at the Academy were beautifully restored, along with six stained-glass windows in the chapel. Even the belltower was reconstructed. And it seems Sister Mary is pleased.

According to a 2002 Boulder *Daily Camera* article on the Academy, Sister Mary's ghost is felt throughout the building. "Sister Mary really likes the Academy building," said an Academy employee. "We had a cook who saw her in the kitchen." It seems as though Sister Mary has blessed the building with her presence. And there has only been one instance when her spirit has been startling. During the renovation a construction worker walked off the job. He told a resident of the Academy that he saw the nun clearly on several occasions and it was getting the best of him.

The Academy has remained true to its founder's vision: a place to help people who are frail of body, feed their minds and nurture their spirits. It seems to be true in more ways than one. ❖

References

Anderson, Christopher. "Forensic advances may solve case." <u>Daily Camera,</u> August 8, 1997.

Barker, Jane Valentine. <u>76 Boulder Historic Homes</u>. Boulder: Pruett Publishing, 1976.

Broysky ,Cindy. "Historic group hopes to scare up funds with ghostly tour on Halloween weekend." <u>Daily Camera,</u> October 27, 1999.

Cornett, Linda. "Boulder's ghosts." <u>Daily Camera</u>. <u>Focus Magazine</u>. October 23, 1977.

Kauder, Carol. "Strolling with the spirits." <u>Daily Camera,</u> October 19, 1999.

Marshall, Julie. "Nurturing spirit," <u>Daily Camera,</u> May 10, 2002.

O'Connor, Kelley. "Ghostly goings-on." <u>Daily Camera</u>. <u>The Sunday Camera Magazine,</u> October 25, 1986.

Peters, Mike. "Ghost Story: Was Boulder house haunted?" <u>Greeley Tribune</u>, October 31, 1984.

Pettem, Silvia. <u>Legend of a Landmark, A History of the Hotel Boulderado</u>. Missoula: Pictorial Histories Publishing, 1997, 2nd ed.

Pierce, J. Kingston. "Our favorite haunts." <u>Daily Camera</u>. <u>The Sunday Camera Magazine,</u> 1985.

Repplier, F.O. <u>As A Town Grows</u>. Boulder: Johnson Publishing, 1959.

Royko, Mark. "The Restless Scout: Boulder's Clinton Dumm stalks the ghostly periphery." <u>Boulder Fall Magazine,</u> 1987

Schamper, SuAnna Jo. "Little Walter's Soft Steps: A young spook still makes the rounds in Montgomery House." <u>Boulder Fall Magazine,</u> 1989.

Seipel, Tracy & Marilyn Robinson. "Murderer to try for parole again." <u>Denver Post</u>, January 24, 1993.

Smith, Phyllis. <u>A Look at Boulder, From Settlement to City.</u> Boulder: Pruett Publishing, 1981.

Whaley, Monte. "A (sixth) sense of community." <u>Denver Post</u>, October 31, 2000.